THE SHENANIGANS

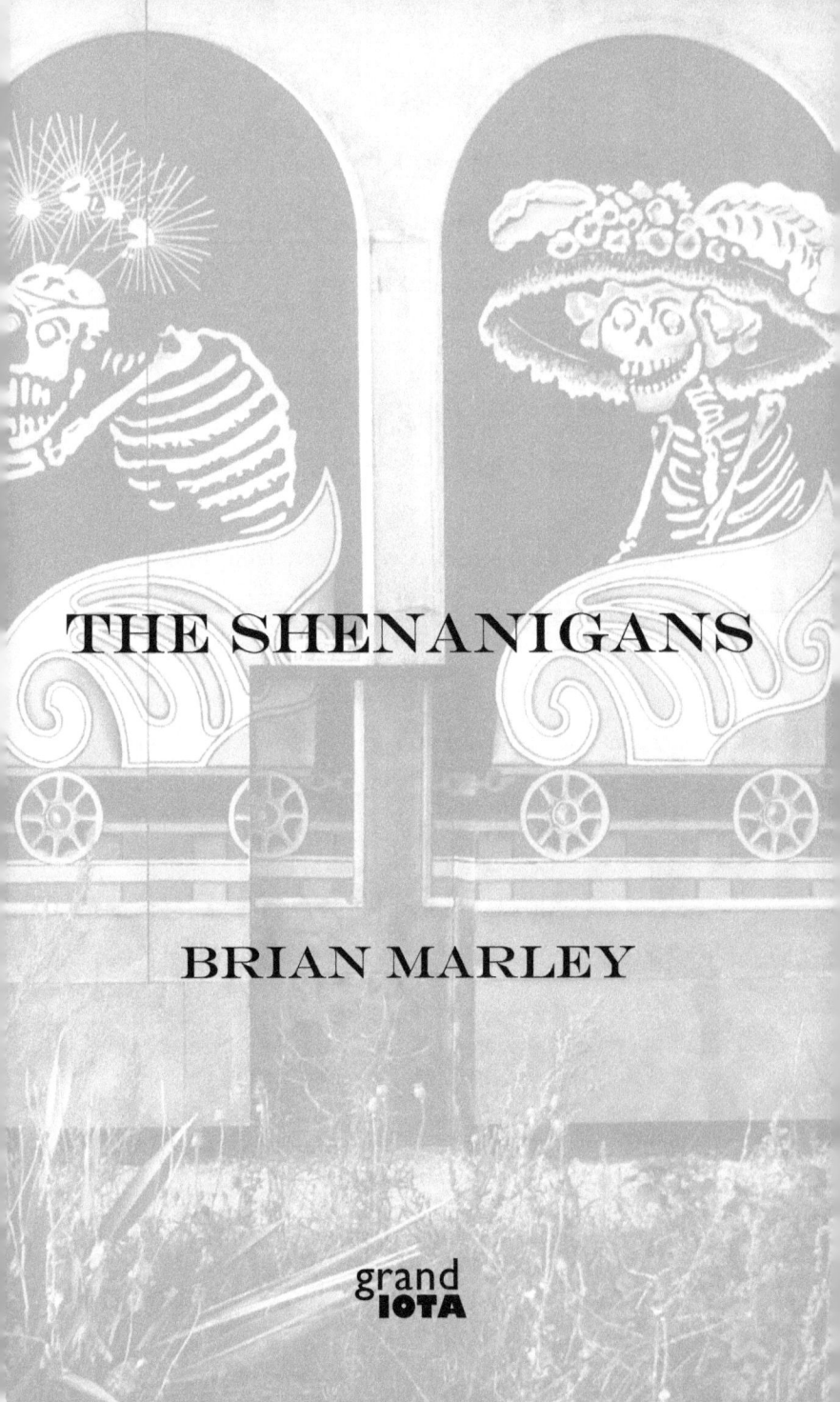

THE SHENANIGANS

BRIAN MARLEY

grand
IOTA

Published by
grand**IOTA**

2 Shoreline, St Margaret's Rd, St Leonards TN37 6FB
&
37 Downsway, North Woodingdean, Brighton BN2 6BD

www.grandiota.co.uk

Typesetting & book design by Reality Street

A catalogue record for this book is available from the British Library

ISBN: 978-1-874400-78-3

My thanks to the editors who published earlier versions
of the following stories:

'Trelawney the Lion-Tamer' – *Stand*

'Wooed' – *Tears in the Fence*

'Garden' – *Kater Murr's Press*

'Aquarium Light', 'A Valedictory Note', 'Running through the City',
'The Siblings Jones' – *Golden Handcuffs Review*

'Democracy', 'An Interrogation', and 'Poultice' were grouped under
the title 'A Perigee Selection' in the anthology *The Alchemist's Mind:
A Book of Narrative Prose by Poets* (Reality Street)

'Jonah' and 'Unnatural Order' were 'scripts' for two digital
animations made in collaboration with Andrew Greaves
(AG Editions)

Special thanks to my critical friends
Lou Rowan & Ken Edwards

Contents

Acknowledgments

I OWE MANY people more than I can say. In some cases, more than I dare to admit. And yet ... How many people does it take to write a book? (That's not the feeder line of a joke, by the way; cast that puerile thought and anticipatory snigger from your mind.) In this case: just one. That's my name on the cover, spine and title page of the slim volume clasped in your hand. But writing is a challenging business, a bit of a slog at times, and occasionally, annoyingly, the word machine grinds to a halt. Whenever problems of that nature have occurred, as all too often they have in recent years, I've been inundated with offers of help, much of which has transitioned seamlessly from word to deed. According to my publisher (nagging me incessantly, as publishers are inclined to do), failing to acknowledge such acts of kindness would be remiss, an all-too-typical example of authorial ingratitude – though writers, stung by such criticism, thwok the ball back over the net by saying it's publishers, not writers, who are the world's worst ingrates. Love all. Let's move on.

⊖

Stella, my dear sweet girl, I can't thank you enough for the emergency loan of your spare prosthetic limb when mine, of a sudden, fell apart. A surprisingly snug fit it was too, all things considered. Because your foot is considerably daintier than mine, I crumpled up the front page of *The Times* and wedged it in the toecap of my shoe. To level me up, I used two UK size 9 charcoal-imbued insoles and a half-inch shoe lift, layering them in those roomy tan wingtips you always said you liked.

Which reminds me: what excellent taste you have!

I often mull over why we divorced. Two authors, both of whom have had a leg amputated just below the right knee, though for different reasons. We were, were we not, a match made in Heaven? And if I've said it once I've said it a thousand times, though you won't listen: those other women meant nothing to me, absolutely nothing!

Anyway, with leg strapped in place, socks pulled up, lift and insoles inserted and shoes tightly laced, negotiating the stands, stairs and stage at the Frankfurt Book Fair was an absolute breeze. I bestrode the event like a colossus and the chafing was minimal.

⊖

Three years ago, while hospitalised (the result of an accident rather than illness – I'll explain later), hence unable to conduct my own research, my agent, Tandy Baume, queen of contracts, a formidable negotiator, card sharp and cigarillo smoker, engaged on my behalf (unbeknown to me, I was in a coma at the time) the best researcher in all of Muswell Hill, a London suburb crammed to bursting with researchers, most of whom are unable to find employment in their chosen field and must of needs eke out a living as baristas in coffee shops, of which, in the vicinity, there are scores, perhaps hundreds. His name: Finbar McCracken. Tandy refers to him as Fin the Firecracker.

Confession time: I would not have been able to lard 'A Valedictory Note' with so many keen insights into the workings of the British secret services were it not for Fin's indefatigable delvings into the published and unpublished accounts of former operatives, few, scattered and heavily redacted though they are, and his brief but telling interview with the man known to fellow secret service ops as Kenton Faecalmatter. Now residing in the Forest of Dean – though not in a house, as one might expect, but bivouacked deep in the forest itself – Faecalmatter lives almost exclusively on nuts, berries, and during his brief nocturnal forays into Ross-on-Wye, scraps from discarded take-away cartons – a diet that has dealt his cancer a knockout blow, so he claims.

The various classified documents found by Fin in the Deep Web (whatever that is – a technophobic author can't know everything) proved invaluable during the writing of 'A Valedictory Note'. And his unexpectedly intimate street knowledge of Matlock was of considerable help when, due to tiresome but unavoidable teaching commitments in Australia (can creative writing be taught? apparently not), I was unable to visit the town.

Fin's boyfriend, Stelios – who is, I gather, a linchpin of London's small but thriving community of experimental versifiers (a community hermetically sealed against mass media interest, which is why you won't have heard of him) – also happens to bake a delicious moussaka, his signature dish. Fin favours stir fries, mainly of Taiwanese origin. A case of fine wine, sparkling conversation and rapier wit were my contributions to the meals we've shared in their, as their landlord put it, 'surprisingly spacious bijou apartment' (tiny is how I'd describe it, despite the astronomically high rent they pay).

⊖

Fin has just sent me this: *The Deep Web (also known as the Dark Web, Deepnet, Invisible, Secret and Hidden Web) comprises sites that can't be tracked by internet search engines.* It is, it seems, from what he says, a place where paedophiles exchange sickening images that encourage the genital stimulation of self and others. Also where contract killings are arranged, often of, by and for suspected paedophiles, or by lone vigilantes and international law enforcement agents posing as paedophiles, some of whom are probably closet paedophiles. Fin says it's wall-to-wall paedophiles in there, almost as many as there are men currently living on this planet, hence in the entire solar system and beyond, as, for better or worse, we seem to be alone. So now I know but rather wish I didn't.

$$\ominus$$

As usual, I have my accountant Chester Stapleton to thank for sorting out the gross financial mismanagement and outright criminality that occurred on the watch of his rat-faced predecessor; that and negotiating tirelessly with the voracious bloodsuckers at HM Revenue & Customs over what they claim are taxes underpaid in 2015-18. Absolute nonsense! I paid my taxes in full, I've got receipts to prove it (though HM Revenue & Customs say they're fakes).

But really, what can one do?

What Chester does, and does supremely well.

While HMRC and the Crown Prosecution Service weigh up the evidence, behind the scenes Chester has gradually been turning tax evasion (illegal) into tax avoidance (not illegal, just unethical – heigh-ho, I can live with that). He's a tax loophole wizard, rightly held in awe by his fellow accountants.

His predecessor, whom my solicitor has made me promise not to name while criminal investigations are underway ... oh, what the hell, he's called Barry Upwith, of the City of London firm, since dissolved, Lark, Upwith & Lark. Their corporate slogan, 'Up with the Larks', was so cringeworthy I really should have taken my business elsewhere, but didn't, fool that I am. Lark and Lark (married to each other and happily, so I gather) are blameless in this matter and have since relocated to Guernsey to start afresh. I wish them well. Upwith, according to Fin, is developing property in Venezuela on land bought with monies – mine! (and, to be fair, that of at least twenty others) – that had been set aside for tax purposes. Chester is using the strong possibility of extradition and criminal proceedings being brought against Upwith to stall HMRC.

In the acknowledgments to my next book, a true crime novel entitled *Crime, My Destiny*, I hope to be able to report that this matter has been resolved to the dissatisfaction of Barry Upwith and the immense satisfaction of all other parties concerned.

In partial lieu of payment for services rendered, I agreed to immortalise Chester on the printed page. Several of his favourite tattoos appear in 'Trelawney the Lion-Tamer'. But, temperamentally, Chester is not in the least like sweet, addled Trelawney. Rather, his sheer bloody-minded no-holds-barred ruthlessness in pursuit of his goal, whatever that goal may be, informs the character of bat hospicer and art photographer Charles 'Blood' l'Orange in 'Running through the City' – of which, because of rather than despite l'Orange's chilling weirdness, Chester is inordinately proud. It takes, as they say, all sorts. He's pre-ordered fifty copies of *The Shenanigans* to give to family, friends and foes, mainly foes, and asked me to sign them and include in the personalised dedication (I've been given a list of recipients, whose names I'm not at liberty to divulge) the phrase 'Chester is l'Orange with knobs on'. To which, of course, I've acquiesced.

He also told me about a chance sexual encounter in a pantomime horse. Accurate, he insists, in every detail; the implication being that he was one of the two participants. With his permission, I've adapted the situation for 'Trelawney'.

⊖

Kudos to Tony Oakley, Senior Research Director at Camberwell Prostheticus UK, for suggesting that I have a new limb made, one with a pressure-sensitive foot. He engineered a prototype, which I've been testing for the last couple of months, and the results are, to say the least, encouraging. Apparently there are things called pressure transducers in the foot which send signals to electrodes set in the stump which are interpreted by the stump nerves and translated into gait. I hope I've got that right; he'll let me know if I haven't. One of the side effects is, however, something I'd never experienced with my previous prosthesis, nor the one Stella loaned me – an infuriating itch in the arch of the foot, near, if this were flesh and bone, the medial metatarsals. I can't scratch the itch because, needless to say, it's imaginary, an atypical phantom limb pain. Upon removing the limb, the itch vanishes.

Tony's solution to this problem was to design an electronic scratch, a device no bigger than a one-pound coin. Pressing the button in the middle of the device initiates a five-second scratch, providing temporary relief.

At least that's what I thought was happening.

Recently he admitted, somewhat sheepishly, that the electronic scratch doesn't actually do anything. It's a placebo. But even though I know this to be true, when I press the button the itching stops. The human mind really is a strange and wonderful thing.

While chatting during adjustments to the prosthesis, Tony mentioned (I can't recall how the topic came up, but I'm glad it did) that his great grandfather spent several months working as a doctor in a gold-mining town by the name of Vulture City, long since abandoned, in Arizona. Though I've changed nearly every aspect of what he told me, and situated 'Wooed' in one of the UK's most isolated towns (I won't say where), circa 1950, it retains a heady whiff of frontier life (and death) rendered as a fever dream.

$\ominus$

Perhaps this is as good a time as any to reveal how I lost my leg. The subject invariably comes up during interviews and I get so tired of repeating the facts I've taken to embellishing them in various ways – for my own amusement if nothing else. Newspaper arts and culture editors tend to publish my utterances unquestioningly, no matter what I say, even though I once claimed to have had my appendix removed during an alien abduction. The press love outré statements, the more flagrantly outré the better. But some key facts have never been told. Here, then, is the definitive version. I'll have Tandy, whose idea this was, add it to the press kit.

On second thoughts ... what actually happened is so boring I'm likely to fall asleep before I've managed to write it down.

Instead, place a cross in the box by the explanation you like the best. Once you've made your choice, stick with it through thick and thin, hell and high water. Don't be swayed by the choices others have made, even if those others gang up on you at dinner parties and try to make you change your mind; even if they send you to Coventry or somewhere worse, assuming there is somewhere worse. Remember, there's no right or wrong explanation; this isn't a test of your intelligence or credulity.

Let's begin.

I lost my right leg when I was ...

❏ kicked in the shin while trying to secure a drunken horse to a lamp post outside the Co-op in Appleby-in-Westmorland during the final day of the town's annual horse fair.

❑ stricken with necrotising fasciitis following what should have been a routine ingrown toenail operation.

❑ savaged by a rottweiler that came [cliché alert!] out of nowhere, or, more precisely, out of a boat house on the shores of Lake Maggiore, whereupon my lower leg spontaneously detached in a manner not dissimilar to how lizards shed their tails when under attack. The dog was so startled by this turn of events it sped off, my leg clamped in its powerful jaws.

❑ struck by lightning while [a] climbing a tree in Windsor Great Park to retrieve a crying child's balloon, or [b] paragliding over the Grand Canyon, or [c] playing celebrity golf on the Eden Roc Cap Cana course in the Dominican Republic with Bill Murray and Alice Cooper, both of whom were shocked but otherwise unscathed.

❑ bitten by a common death adder while hiking in woodland near the town of Tweed Heads, New South Wales. The anti-venom, though injected immediately, proved to be counterfeit and only marginally effective because the active ingredient had been adulterated with who-knows-what-cheap-substitute by a criminal gang in Lucknow.

❑ either [a] caught in a bear trap in the wilds of Nova Scotia, or [b] mangled by the jaws of a combine harvester while I was napping in a cornfield after a hard day writing sonnets.

❏ mauled by a great white shark in an unprovoked attack – the first of its kind to occur off the coast of Pembrokeshire. The shark, not native to those waters and a very long way from home, was presumed to have escaped or been released from the illegally-held private collection of a wealthy amateur elasmobranchologist.

❏ hit by a train (that didn't stop) after I rolled down an embankment and onto the line, having been struck a glancing blow by a large vehicle (a cement lorry, I think, which also failed to stop) while walking along the hard shoulder of the unlit road running parallel to the tracks. My Audi had broken down ten minutes earlier. Having no mobile phone, torch, tools or mechanical knowhow, I had no option but to hoof it to the nearest service station, a glimmer in the distance, to seek help.

Plenty of spurious explanations to choose from. Take your pick.

I hope never to have occasion to speak of this again.

⊖

To Spitz Warner Dental Solutions for emergency

repairs to my shattered (olive pit) upper plate, the absence of which would have made my speech to the English Goldfish Society, 'Colonel Esquivel's Major Regret', and a preliminary reading of the story 'Aquarium Light', unintelligible. That the EGS paid handsomely for my time and effort, promptly at that, and the following week sent round a complimentary fish tank, is testament to the kindness and courtesy with which they treat their guest speakers. The tank is situated on a small table in my library. I've filled it with rocks and raked gravel in emulation of a Japanese Zen garden, the one at Ryoanji, and it never fails to inspire my quest for the mot juste and the perfect sentence.

⊖

To Air India, which mislaid my suitcase en route to a literary festival in New Delhi. The following morning the airline delivered a case to my hotel which, although identical to mine, and although my name was on the handler's tag, turned out to belong to someone else. Luckily, the combination lock hadn't been changed from the factory setting (9999). No clues within as to whose suitcase I'd received, but as I had Mr Unknown's case it's possible – nay, probable – that he had mine. A disaster? You'd think so. But the clothes I unpacked were a perfect fit and of superior quality. Good colour combinations, too. Needless to say, I vetoed the underwear, as would any self-respecting fussbudget. Neither Mr Unknown nor I – I think I can speak on his behalf – reported the mix-up, and the airline's mistake was never rectified. Presumably he was as pleased with my wardrobe as I was with his.

⊖

To Mr Unknown: I apologise for discarding your shaving kit, underwear, and leather slippers (two sizes too small, alas). But those nitroglycerin tablets – which I recognised immediately because I too have angina – came in handy. If only you'd been able to say the same. By mistake, my mind on a hundred other things, I'd packed an empty pill dispenser in my suitcase, which became, because of the mix-up, your suitcase. I only realised what I'd done when I returned home and found a bottle of tablets, its seal unbroken, in the bathroom cabinet. I do hope you didn't have urgent need of them.

⊖

To Sparky Wellbrook Jr, of Sparky's Taxis, Brixton, my charioteer of choice, whose real name rather than *nom-de-cab* is Errol, plain old Errol. The Sparky's Taxi number is first call when I have reason to travel swiftly and comfortably to a location within the M25, and occasionally, on expenses, beyond. Errol's dedication to duty is such that I'm reminded of Greyfriars

Bobby, the Skye terrier immortalised in Edinburgh's Old Town, who guarded his master's grave for fourteen years until he too expired.

Errol isn't quite as stalwart as that.

But almost.

Late last August, for example, he waited outside the Groucho Club on double yellow lines from early afternoon Friday to late morning Monday while I caroused within. I'd said with confidence that I'd be an hour or two, three at the most. More fool me. During his lonely vigil he peed into an empty 2.0 litre bottle of Clearview Still Spring Water as discreetly as one can on a busy London thoroughfare; clenched his buttocks while chanting the cabbies' antidiarrheal mantra, *Pepto-Bismol, Pepto-Bismol*; and drove round the block in first gear whenever a traffic warden shimmied into view. Because he didn't dare leave the cab unattended, he subsisted on takeaway margheritas courtesy of Pizza Pilgrims, further up Dean Street, and Deliveroo.

My fellow carousers were the publisher and editor in chief of the up-and-coming house Picard-Hoy (a decidedly fathead minnow since gobbled up by a freshwater shark), neither of whom, when I rang the following week, could recall the precise details of our meeting, in particular their boundless enthusiasm for *The Shenanigans* and their wish to publish it under what I thought, and gently reminded them, were favourable terms for all concerned. A glance at the copyright page will show you that I took my business elsewhere, and Errol and I came, as always, to an amicable agreement about the fare and the tip – substantial in both cases, but well earned.

⊖

To Simeon Fischer and the staff at Poltroons, the most exclusive gourmet restaurant in all of West London, its location known to very few people, even fewer of whom have had the privilege of eating there. Entry is by invitation only, and no exceptions are made to this rule, no matter how famous you are. Even Nelson Mandela was turned away, which caused a minor diplomatic incident.

While being driven from your home to the restaurant and back again by a tight-lipped Poltroon employee, you'll be blindfolded. This, and the dizzying route undertaken in getting you from A to B, is a necessary precaution.

If Simeon gives you a call, don't, whatever you do, say no. Unless you're a top celebrity, he won't call again. And just think what you would be missing. The organic *non-alcoholic* whiskey sour that cocktail mixmeister Jaimie Fuller makes is, for example, a stunning creation. And the imaginatively varied menus, using nothing but seasonally available, locally sourced produce foraged from skips at the back of Sainsbury, Tesco, Waitrose, Asda and other supermarket chains, are created by none other than the infamous Maximus Keele, former TV chef, former alcoholic, former bankrupt, former rough sleeper, whose self-destructive and appalling behaviour, as revealed in his highly entertaining ghost-written memoir, *Leaping the Gorge*, led me, with his permission, to touch on one of his less salubrious exploits in 'Running through the City'.

I ghosted *Leaping the Gorge* for free, and indeed, why not? Though we lost contact during the worst of his oblivion years, Max has always been a great friend. Admittedly, he's volatile, a tad unreliable when his medications are in need of adjustment, occasionally violent in word and deed, but he's never, ever ungrateful or uncharitable. *One of nature's double-barrelled sweethearts*, my father once said of him. Max and I have downed many a whisky sour in the wee small hours at Poltroons, and I hope to down many more with him in the years to come. *Salut, my friend!*

⊖

To my estimable PA, Marian Fishborne, for managing my diary, typing up my handwritten work, forging my signature (with, of course, my permission) on various documents, cheques and stock replies to fan letters, and, most important of all, preparing my writing room. Those of you who've read my *Paris Review* interview will be aware that writing is, to my way of thinking, a ritualised struggle with the English language, and the circumstances have got to be just right if I've the slightest chance of winning that struggle.

First, a pinch of sea salt is deposited in each corner of the room, which, by the way, has been soundproofed almost to anechoic chamber standards. The intention being to keep at bay the city's fearsome din and its limitless reserves of negative energy. Marian then decants a small quantity of my morning urine into a perfume atomiser, which is used to purify the air and establish the 'right' atmosphere, i.e., pheremonally conducive to sustained creative thought. Then and only then do I enter the room, dressed in a silk kimono, woolly hat, fingerless gloves, and grey felt carpet slippers (no socks).

The pages I completed the day before, now typed, sit on an occasional table by a lectern in the centre of the room, though I rarely feel the need to consult them. I keep it all in my head – every word, however small, and every last punctuation mark. Stacked on the lectern are ten sheets – always ten, neither more nor fewer – of Original Crown Mill Cream Vellum Paper. On the lectern's lower lip rests an F. Scott Fitzgerald Writers Limited Edition fountain pen, made by Montblanc. Situated five paces behind the lectern is a chaise longue upholstered in green velvet upon which, occasionally, I recline to mull over certain phrases before committing them to paper. Sometimes, while mulling, I take a brief, refreshing nap. There's a commode in one corner of the room should nature need to be satisfied. Ah, I almost forgot the most important thing: I write entirely in the dark to avoid distractions. The mere sight of my hand guiding the pen can stifle a valuable thought or send it completely awry. Even signing my name is difficult unless I close my eyes tight, the way one makes a wish as a child while blowing out the candles on a birthday cake.

Over the years, Marian has become wonderfully adept at transcribing my sightless scrawls and accidental overscrawls into the singing/stinging lines that readers of my work have come to know and love. The writing day is done when all ten sheets have been filled. Sometimes that may take as little as two or three hours, in which case I sheathe my pen and repair to one of the local bistros for something to eat. If things aren't going well, Marian knocks discreetly on the door at 2.00pm and wordlessly (so as not to break my train of thought) places a tray containing a thermos flask of Earl Grey and a plate of cucumber sandwiches on a dresser to the left of the door.

If necessary this procedure is repeated at 7.00pm, though the evening repast is different, usually consisting of lightly buttered oatcakes and gorgonzola cheese, plus a very large gin and tonic (with ice and lemon).

Sometimes, refreshing the atmosphere mid-afternoon with a fine mist of urine boosts the creative process and spurs me on. Needless to say, I don't leave the room until all ten pages have been filled. Nor does Marian go home. She stays until I finish, usually before midnight but sometimes later, much later. Because I pay her well, I assume she has a home to go to, and a husband, perhaps even children, grown-up children who find the family nest much too well-feathered to leave except for an occasional Mummy-funded holiday at an exclusive foreign resort. Curiously, I've never thought to ask.

⊖

'Don't complain, don't explain,' said Gore Vidal. Easier said than done. It would be foolish to deny the fact that all professional writers' lives are bestrewn with traps, sometimes set accidentally but more often than not maliciously. Mine is no exception. Jealousy and envy dog my every step. Here, in no particular order of detestation, are my would-be nemeses: Scott Hopkins (vinegar dispenser); Phillip Mates (hornswoggler); Richard Poppleton (naysayer); Fanny Flintoff (gossipmonger); Sir Charles Forcemeat (pool pisser); Tom Stapleton (wrong footer); Tootie McTait (ambuscader); Mimi ap Evans (persiflager); Tim Fortesque (dream crusher); Babbity Dowser (foot dragger); and Wee Willy Wendle (caboodler). If I must, post mortem, be cast headlong into Satan's fiery pit, I fully expect to find them there, Poppleton, Dowser, Flintoff and the gang, stewing for all eternity in their own rancid juices.

⊖

But why end on a sour note when there's so much in life worth celebrating? Such as the fact that none of our children, Stella's and mine, have become writers, hence our competitors, though Gregor has achieved fame as a translator of technical manuals, his masterpiece (it won a major literary award!) being the German→English (he's also, by the way, fluent in Swedish, French and Italian) workshop service book of the Volkswagen VS TDI R-Line JE DESIGN Widebody Touareg, a top of the range model introduced in 2011 which boasts a powerful 4.1 litre V8 engine. What made Gregor's work stand out for the judges of the PEN Translation Prize was that the German→English was rendered in sestinas, the execution of which was so subtle that initially only a handful of savvy versifiers recognised what he'd done. It kick-started the engine of revolution in the hitherto stalled world of technical translation.

Haynes, the world's leading publisher of illustrated car maintenance manuals, has since commissioned Gregor to translate into various traditional verse forms the manuals of a dozen German vintage motorcycles and classic cars – including the 1955 Horex Resident Model 8 motorcycle, and Hitler's favourite ride, the Mercedes-Benz 770 W150 cabriolet – and has launched a sister press, Haynes Arts, to showcase these 'highly creative yet eminently practical translations', each of which is limited to five hundred numbered copies, bound in tooled calfskin and signed in the ink equivalent of engine oil by the translator. 'Sumptuous coffee table books for poetry lovers and auto connoisseurs' is how Haynes Arts describe their publications.

Gregor is currently hard at work for another publisher on the maintenance manual of the Ford Anglia E04A 2-door saloon, introduced in 1939, rendering it into Elizabethan English, that of Shakespeare, Marlowe and their contemporaries. Each section of the manual will be presented as a soliloquy in blank verse, concluding, for dramatic effect, with a rhyming couplet.

He is, as such, a literary innovator, and scores of poetech manualists (as, for some unaesthetic reason, they wish to be known) have bobbed merrily along in his wake. His work has been lauded by James Wood, Harold Bloom and other critical heavyweights, and is taught on the *Nouveau-Nouveau Roman and Post-Postmodern* module at the University of East Anglia's School of Literature, Drama and Creative Writing, as well as at Brown University, Rhode Island, and even the Sorbonne. But the accolade of which Gregor is most proud is that of having been made guest of honour at several of the monthly meetings of Oulipo (the Ouvroir de Littérature Potentielle, or workshop of potential literature) at which Jacques Jouet, Harry Mathews and Étienne Lécroart were present, following which the Oulipians, sensing that he was a kindred spirit, invited him to join their ranks. Being extremely shy, and someone who holds fast to Groucho Marx's dictum that 'I wouldn't want to belong to any club that would accept me as a member', Gregor felt obliged to decline, though with, I could tell, considerable regret.

Because I'm inordinately proud of him – as indeed I am of his siblings, Rhetta, an architect, and Coryn, a tree surgeon – I can easily overlook the fact that he nearly killed me (the accident I alluded to several pages earlier). For which he has since apologised, sincerely and profusely. There we were, shoulder to shoulder in the kitchenette of his tiny Pimlico flat, chopping root vegetables for a hearty winter stew, when he had one of his 'galvanic' (as he refers to them) spasms, a massive amplification of the slight tremor that has afflicted him since birth. As usual, we'd been arguing about something and nothing; about whether there's *always* a pot of gold at the end of *every* rainbow or whether there was only ever *one pot* at the end of the *very first* rainbow. I can't recall which of those idiotic notions I favoured, but according to Laetitia, Gregor's fiancé, we were arguing fiercely and more than a little drunkenly, slurring our words and embellishing them with violent gestures, a particularly dangerous thing to do given the limited space in the kitchenette and the razor-sharp implements we held in our hands.

Next thing I knew, I was in hospital, waking up from a 'long sleep' (O how medics love their euphemisms!). According to my consultant, Mr Ghosh, for almost three months I'd been unconscious and unresponsive (the worst possible indicator on the Glasgow

Coma Scale) and perpetually on the cusp of brain death. Because it was mistakenly noted in the hospital records that I was a Catholic rather than a Jew, a priest had been summoned not once but twice to issue the Viaticum. On the second occasion, Laetitia found him mumbling by my bedside, wooden cross in one hand, the other marking the air with ritualistic gestures, and sent him packing.

Although it's not uncommon for former coma patients to say they could hear everything said about and to them, but were unable even to twitch an eyebrow in response, I heard nothing. Not a sausage. Instead, my locked-in mind conjured up the story 'Running through the City', and I entered into it and lived through every moment of it again and again, hundreds of times, taking the part of each of the characters in turn, seeing their world entirely through their eyes. As the realisation of a journey to the afterlife, stripped of spells but rich in metaphor, I would contend that it puts the *Egyptian Book of the Dead* and other ancient funerary texts to shame.

Laetitia later told me what had happened in the kitchenette. Awakened from an afternoon nap by raised and querulous voices, she saw me dealt a glancing blow from the blunt edge of Gregor's cleaver. No major harm done; a hefty bruise in the making, that's all. Trouble was, I hadn't seen it coming and was knocked off balance. I toppled over, arms flailing, and cracked my skull on the polished marble floor. Blood everywhere. An ambulance was quickly summoned. Emergency treatment was given to relieve pressure on the brain, followed, three days later, by a second, similar procedure. Within a few hours of that my condition stabilised. But then came cardiac arrest and, almost immediately, a stroke – I won't bore you with the details. That I survived is remarkable. Even more remarkable is that within eighteen months I'd made a full recovery.

Whereas Tandy attributes my survival to a thick skull and sheer good fortune, I attribute it to Joanna, my girlfriend at the time, now my wife, who slept on a pallet by my bedside for weeks on end and patiently wooed me back to health. Everyone likes a happy ending, so I'm told, and I'm more than happy to oblige. *The Shenanigans* is dedicated to her with – and really, what could be more appropriate? – undying love.

The Elements

EARTH APPLAUDS WHEN water stands up for itself, takes
a deep breath and bursts into flames.

Running through the City

1. The Mercurial

> The run has taken place annually since Medieval times. Its purpose: to guarantee strong trade and a bumper harvest in the coming year. Legend has it that if the runner fails to complete the course the city will sicken and die.
> – Edwin Gong-Fermor, *Living Myths & Legends*

I HAD BEEN chosen to run through the city with a flaming torch in the dead of night. A drab, post-industrial city. Winter solstice: the longest night. Beyond the confines of the town hall square a strict curfew had been imposed. Every light citywide had been doused: domestic lighting, shop window displays, streetlamps, billboards – absolutely everything. Even traffic lights and the emergency exit signs in public buildings.

Overwhelmed by the occasion, the moon hid its face behind clouds.

My torch, flickering and sputtering as I ran, its yellow flame leaning backwards, over my left shoulder, was the city's only source of illumination. As indeed it should be. Yet somehow, in all that darkness, I lost my way. I'd memorised the route; had walked it one hundred times or more, then dozens of times more with my eyes closed, tapping the ground ahead of me with a white stick borrowed from a neighbour, counting my steps and dividing them by two to take into account a runner's extended stride. I knew the height of every kerb. Every item of street furniture was known to me. The distance between intersections had been carefully paced and committed to memory.

For several weeks prior to running with the torch I dreamt of nothing else – dreams so vivid I woke lathered in sweat, utterly exhausted. Those dreams I incorporated into my training regime. I walked the designated route ten times by day, one hundred times by night. But it wasn't enough. Despite all this meticulous preparation, I strayed.

The runners in recent years had been medal-winning sportsmen whose track and field careers were drawing to a close. Though once, unaccountably and disastrously, a celebrity chef was chosen. I was neither of those things. A decade ago I came careering out of nowhere to rank 24th on the International Tennis Federation's pro circuit. A fluke, nothing but. I played a succession of top-rank players when they were at their lowest ebb, struggling variously with flu, wrist and ankle sprains, gastro-enteritis, depression, bunions, migraine and hives. The following year, when I returned to nowhere, nowhere embraced me. It has held me fast ever since. That 24th ranking was my sole claim to fame.

Until now.

A neighbour – not Henry, the partially sighted one who loaned me the stick, another one – suggested that, ancient ranking aside, I'd been chosen because of my powerful left arm. Like many a tennis player, the triceps and biceps of my primary racquet arm are overdeveloped, but it's the muscle groups in the shoulder, chest, neck and back, the trapezius, deltoids, pectoralis and suchlike, where the difference is noticeable. I'm a little lopsided is what I'm saying. More than that: the way I fill a shirt is peculiar. A girlfriend said I was a divided being: left half Charles Atlas, right half the 90lb weakling who got sand kicked in his face, perhaps by Atlas himself. Needless to say, as a girlfriend she didn't last long. But my neighbour had a point: 'Mile after mile,' he said, 'the torch has to be held high, and according to your predecessors it weighs a fucking ton. Every mile you run adds another pound to its weight. Because you're not allowed to rest or even change hands, an incredibly strong arm is required.' That's precisely what I've got.

Yes, the torch is heavy, and the wind, gustier than the Met Office predicted, occasionally licks the flame against my face, singeing my left ear and frizzling the wiry tufts of hair that grow out of it. But what's causing me the most grief is the costume I'm obliged to wear. It's an appallingly poor fit. The winged helmet keeps slipping down over my eyes, restricting visibility, and the all-in-one body suit is perfect for an orangutan – so long in the body the crotch droops almost to my knees, so short in the leg the ankle wings sit mid-calf. Naturally I assumed a mistake had been made, but the events committee representative

who delivered it, a Mr Suleiman, said the costume
had been tailored according to the measurements
provided. 'By whom?' I asked. I hadn't had a fitting.
While obsessively training and memorising the route,
I'd given little thought to what I'd have to wear. He
riffled through dozens of business cards, selected one
and handed it to me:

LIL le MESURIER
Senior Costume Consultant
Citywide Arts

So that's what became of my emphatically dumped
girlfriend!

'The two key considerations,' said Mr Suleiman,
'are DNA prediction and coffin size. The DNA sample
that was extracted from the placental cord when you
were born (you won't remember that happening, you
were far too young and nipple-fixated) enables us to
construct a basic computer profile. We factor in vari-
ables such as diet, exercise, childhood diseases, proximity to environmental hazards, duration and relative
depth of depression caused by unemployment and/or
rocky love life and/or bereavements (if any), other
signs of mental instability, quality of stool and urine
(sampled surreptitiously at six-month intervals over a
three-year period prior to the run – yes, we plan well
ahead), and whether there's a tendency for the chosen
candidate to engage in life/limb-threatening reckless
behaviour, known to actuaries worldwide as the Fuck-
wit Factor. (Your FF rating was just above average, by

the way.) Meanwhile, our resident astrologer works up a chart for you, focusing on the night of the run. Nothing is left to chance but chance itself.'

'I see.' (Though frankly I was none the wiser.) 'What's coffin size?'

'A euphemism.'

'Meaning ...?'

'Forget it, it's hardly worth mentioning. In previous years the candidates were perfectly happy with my explanation. They considered it sufficient unto itself, which it is. They were *grateful*.'

'Nonetheless ...'

Mr Suleiman draws air deep into his lungs. He lets it out slowly, through pursed lips, flexing them as though blowing smoke rings – a vain attempt to buy time and haze the air between us. I wait, maintaining eye contact. 'Your height,' he concedes with a sigh, 'in any given year between birth and death. The size of coffin that would be required if, for example, you died age fourteen. Or fifty. Or with osteoporosis at the age of seventy-nine. Or if you developed diabetes (which can happen at any age), leading to severe circulatory problems and the onset of gangrene, resulting in both legs being amputated somewhere between ankle and knee.'

I say nothing. My eyes, unblinking, bore into his. Proselytising graduates of the Mesmer school extol the virtues of this technique, though seducing women is the use to which it's mostly put, without success.

'Look, what no previous candidate has been told

I'll tell you, but strictly entre nous. An actual coffin is made. Throughout your run it will trundle along on a hearse some thirty metres behind you, for use if you collapse and die en route. An understudy in full costume hugs the bumper of the hearse riding a push-bike. He'll complete the run if, for whatever reason, you cannot. Medics in urban camouflage are posted at key stages, ready to spring into action with a frozen gel pack or a liniment spray or a pick-me-up of some kind. Having treated you with despatch, they'll melt into the shadows. Coffin size – no, I haven't forgotten what you asked me – coffin size isn't just about coffins. In fact, it's not really about coffins at all. The coffin size data influences – though only to a small degree, and only when precise tailoring measurements aren't available, as in this case – the cut and fit of the official costume. Happy now?'

We give the costume serious appraisal, him from across the room, me in the full-length mirror to one side of him. Each can probably guess what the other is thinking. Eventually he says: 'The official photographer will be here soon. Charles 'Blood' l'Orange. As you know, he mainly does fashion shoots: weird, hostile, often deranged-looking women clothes-horsing stitched scraps of blood-spattered car-wreck uphol-stery, their contorted poses framed as if in a visionary bubble. (Think Jeanne d'Arc's ecstasy of pain as the flames licked up her thighs.) His signature backdrop: an urban riot, the kind of riot they have in cities less law-abiding than ours. Sources close to l'Orange hint that he was one of the catalysts for the 2011 disturbances in London and elsewhere, the Bradford and Bristol riots of recent years, and Broadwater Farm as long ago as 1985 (the year he left Northern Ireland on graduating from the mural-painting wing of the UDA). This, one assumes, is mere PR puffery – nothing has been substantiated, no charges have been laid. But don't let that fool you, he's an extremely dangerous man. Presumably you've heard of his *Fashion on the Front Line* series, set in Afghanistan. No? I'm surprised. It was, without fear of exaggeration, breathtakingly audacious! Underwear models on foot patrol, under fire from Taliban snipers. Heavy casualties on both sides. Next day, accusations of reckless endangerment were voiced in the Commons, forcing the resignations of the Chief of the Defence Staff and the Secretary of State for Defence, both of whom had, inexplicably, rubber-stamped l'Orange's project. The media, needless to say, lapped it up, as with everything l'Orange does. And with good reason. Time after time, working with difficult or less than perfect material, in impossible situations, he creates magic. That's what we need' – he indicates my costume, unable to suppress a grimace – 'now more than ever. Magic. Lots of it.'

⊖

During a highly unsatisfactory briefing I had with members of the events committee, a particular phrase cropped up a dozen times or more. Every mention of it was followed by a reverential hush, as though a group amen were to follow. Finding myself alone in the boardroom during a coffee break, I stole a glance at the committee's briefing notes. Note, rather. It read, in full:

Sportsmen are complete and utter boneheads, more boneheaded than dinosaurs, with even tinier brains, and this one is a boneheads' bonehead. Subtlety would be wasted on him. Hammer this phrase into his thick stegoceras skull: FLEET – AS – MERCURY!

That they did.

To no avail.

The official costume makes fleetness impossible. Hobbled by it, I stagger from corner to corner like an arthritic drunk, counting aloud and doing swift mental calculations, converting Olympian strides into their crippled insect equivalents. Because of the wildfire chafing of my upper thighs, between actual crotch and the napalm-drenched, low-slung costume crotch, my pace has slackened considerably. The pain is excruciating. (What was it Mr Suleiman said about Joan of Arc?) But no matter how swift my calculations may be, they're wrong, spectacularly wrong. I know they're wrong because I'm lost.

This is what seems to have happened: I took a wrong turn at the five-way intersection known affectionately as The Bottleneck and lurched into Turnbull

Street rather than Agon Avenue. I think that's what happened. The next corner seemed slightly farther away than I expected, a hard right into the lane bordering the river. At that point I thought I'd miscounted slightly; I still assumed all was well. The next turn, a left, was supposed to follow almost immediately. It did. But I knew something was wrong. Where was the beautifully arched stone bridge leading to Hipswell Wharf? Where were the heritage-style cobblestones that should be underfoot? Not knowing what else to do, on I went. I pounded tarmac for perhaps three hundred yards until the road petered out. There followed, in swift succession, a rubble-strewn demolition site, a traffic island under construction with the consistency of a turnip field, and an elevated border of densely packed shrubs, chosen solely for their prickliness, upon which I stumbled and almost fell. Regaining my footing, I plunged into a snicket barely wider than my shoulders. Pinballing from wall to wall, I held the torch high above my head, to minimise damage. It was obvious that only a hearse as thin and slithery as a snake would be able to pursue me down a snicket as narrow as this – assuming that it *was* pursuing me rather than keeping to the official route. But what of my understudy? Was he still hearse-hugging or had I led him astray? If the latter, and his nerve held, and his handlebars weren't too wide for the mouth of the snicket, he might just manage to catch me up. Was that his bicycle bell I heard in the distance, a desolate sound, the cry of an animal whose mate has fallen to the hunter's gun?

All I could hear apart from the bell was the breath rasping in my lungs, the relentless swish-swish-swish-swish of the costume as it shredded my inner thighs like a fine cheese grater, the farty squelch of sweat-soaked running shoes and the slapping sound the soles of the shoes made on, I think, concrete. Despite the gulped breaths and the dull pain in my chest, I felt curiously hollow inside, as though all major organs other than my lungs had been stripped from my body and left at home, arrayed on the bed in the spare room like a serial killer's mock autopsy.

When I said a moment ago that I'd had a briefing with the events committee, that wasn't strictly true. All of the committee members, including the chair, sent apologies for their absence. Instead, I was met by the chair's acting PA, someone else's research assistant, two clueless, bored interns (one shadowing the other, for training purposes), a weasel-faced mail-room clerk who brazenly composed text messages under the table and never once raised his eyes above it, and, to make up the numbers, a 'janitor', a 'security guard' and a 'road sweeper' (I'm guessing about the last three – they just looked as though they'd fit those roles). Mr Suleiman took the minutes. He at least had the decency to look embarrassed.

As I burst out of the alleyway, someone fell into step beside and slightly behind me. I turned my head but saw no-one. The footfalls and harsh breaths I could hear were, I assumed, my own, echoing from the surrounding buildings. At that moment, not looking where I was going, and unable to see much even if I did, my foot struck something large and heavy and I sprawled face down, hitting the ground hard with my chin, the goatee beard I'd so lovingly cultivated acting as a brake, losing much of its bloom and anchorage as it brought me slithering to a halt. Under the forwardly canted lip of the winged helmet, jammed painfully tight on the bridge of my nose (which, from the blood coursing down my nostrils and onto my upper lip, I had reason to believe was now broken), I saw the torch skid and judder along the flagged path several metres ahead of me, sputtering sparks – a wandering star in an otherwise dark universe.

The flame guttered but, miraculously, the torch stayed lit.

At once, and to my amazement, a shadowy figure scooped up the torch and made off with it. Disentangling myself from the spokes of a bicycle – for that's what had lain in my path and brought me down – I sped after the shadow, or at least I tried to. Within a few stumbling steps I knew pursuit would be impossible. I was, I'd be a fool to deny it, in pretty bad shape.

As the tripped-over bicycle seemed to be in much better condition than I was, I leapt onto the saddle and began to pedal furiously. Despite several broken spokes, and the front wheel being so badly warped that on every revolution the rim ground against one of the forks, producing a shower of sparks, the bike was capable of moving faster than my fastest run.

Gradually I gained on the shadowy figure who'd stolen the torch, and before long I was as close behind him as my understudy should have been behind me. But no matter how hard I pedalled, I couldn't seem to narrow the gap between us.

In the distance I could see the flame bobbing with every step the torch thief took, and as I counted the steps and noted the turns he made to left or right, I realised he was assiduously following the route in my head, the route I'd walked, memorised and converted to a runner's pace. It was almost as though I were steering him by mind alone, as though he'd become, in some obscure and troubling way, me. And, like me, he was lost. He was running the wrong way down all the wrong streets, which meant disaster was all but inevitable.

I wondered how long it would be before he ran into a brick wall, thinking the road ahead was, according to his (i.e., my) calculations, clear.

⊖

L'Orange arrived at the photo shoot with three raven-haired, black-clad assistants but without a single item of photographic equipment.

'I want,' he said, swatting away Mr Suleiman's polite enquiry about the absence of a camera, 'to assess the subject thoroughly prior to capturing him.' L'Orange had been dipping into the fancy dress box. He wore a black Zorro mask and a short black cape trimmed with red velvet, and he had the kind of thin waxed moustaches that are designed for villainous twirling. His jet-black (obviously dyed) hair was slicked to his skull, front to back. The effect should have been comical, and it was; but he was so dead of eye, and there was something so chillingly shark-like about his demeanour, that the laughter stuck in my throat.

'Furthermore,' he said, his harsh Belfast accent like two great millstones grinding the words between them, 'I want to capture his essence. That will require more than just a simple series of stills. We, that is, I' – he snapped his fingers and his assistants shuffled meekly from the room, quietly closing the door behind them – 'will capture him in situ during the run. He will run in fear of his life, as he has never run before, as the straggler antelope flees in panic before the salivating jaws of the lion.'

Mr Suleiman, disconcerted by this turn of events, said, 'Maestro, if I may remind you, your contract stipulates that –'

'Stop! Not another word. It's common knowledge that I've never – *never!* – taken heed of such foolishness, yet I've never been sued for breach of contract. Why, you may ask, is that? Let's not pussyfoot. *Because the art I make is of startling originality and its quality is incomparable.* Everyone is satisfied. Even those who hate it have something worth hating. Every death threat I receive – and there are many, more than you can possibly imagine – I take as a compliment.

Despite which, you dare to try me with this nonsense about contractual stipulations! The committees that draw up these contracts know nothing of art; they and their so-called specialist advisers are imbeciles, best ignored. Thus I ignore them. Now step aside, or preferably outside, I wish to observe this, this utterly dismal specimen' – waving a hand in my general direction – 'in all its soul-withering peculiarity.'

So saying, he snapped his fingers in an imperious manner and turned his back on us.

After a moment's hesitation, Mr Suleiman departed in high dudgeon, leaving l'Orange and me together.

⊖

Although I couldn't seem to gain on the torch thief, no matter how hard I pedalled, my mind was gradually catching up with itself, reconciling what should be with what is. I wondered: was the torch thief actually my understudy? A not unreasonable assumption. The bicycle I'd tripped over, every inch of it painted stealth-bomber black, camouflaged for nocturnal and nefarious use, suggested that was the case. Was my understudy resentful of his subordinate role? Was he a former tennis pro, superior to me in skill but whom I'd trounced on serve alone at a major tournament in a whirlwind match lasting less than forty minutes while he was suffering from what sports psychologists call, in their infinite wisdom and for want of a scientific term, the collywobbles? If so, surely he'd be not just singly but doubly resentful, and doubly vengeful too, a man driven to the brink of insanity by a festering hatred. Were I and the collywobbles the principal reasons for his downfall, along with crack cocaine, pole dancers and alimony payments to three grasping former wives (who between them had littered a crèche-full of dependent children)? Putting all that aside, and more to the point, did he consider his subordinate role insulting and embarrassing? If so, would he seize this once-in-a-lifetime opportunity to recapture lost glory by ambushing me and completing the run in my stead?

How could he not.

But then I remembered what l'Orange had to say, thrusting his face aggressively towards me so our brows almost touched. A terrible, suffocating heat radiated from his skin. On his breath a whiff of, I think, hemlock. Neither of us blinked or spoke. Against my will I found myself breathing in sync with him, though his every breath seemed to be deeper than mine, crammed with oxygen, maintaining a stately eupnoea, whereas almost immediately I began to hyperventilate and become agitated. After a minute or two the tension became unbearable. The air between us crackled with static, real or imaginary. I felt an irresistible urge to kiss him on the lips, a brutal, teeth-shattering kiss, just to break this toxic spell, and if he kissed me back and his tongue searched for mine I'd bite it off and spit it in his face.

That's what I wanted to do. It's what I wanted more than anything in the world. But revulsion and fear got the better of me. I closed my eyes to hold back welling tears and my wildfire courage folded in on itself until it was stifled.

I was, however, still furious with Mr Suleiman, furious that he had allowed himself to be driven from the room by the tiny bit of friction generated by l'Orange's finger and thumb. No, not just friction, something more: friction and a small displacement of air. But even so. Not that I could claim to be braver or bolder than him. L'Orange had me exactly where he wanted me. This, verbatim, in Mr Suleiman's absence, is what he said:

'Most artists suffer for their art, but not me. Oh no, not me. What kind of fool do you take me for? *You – you* will suffer on my behalf, for the good of my art. It's a noble undertaking. I guarantee trials and tribulations, more than you think you can bear, but bear them you must. I'll make something of you even if, in so doing, I end up killing you. And why not? Death in the making of art lends the work weight, gravitas. That's my credo. Any common-or-garden psychopath would recognise the truth of it. The greatest artists are, however, without exception, not ordinary psychopaths but supreme ones, so few in number there's only one alive at any one time. That's me.'

There was more, lots more. Despite the sheer unloveliness of his voice, l'Orange clearly adored the sound of it. As he negotiated the jarring shifts between self-preening and menace, something happened – the room began to spin and darken. I think I must have fainted. My next recollection is of being lowered gently onto the chaise longue by Mr Suleiman, who removed my winged helmet and had me sip from a glass of iced water. In that moment, all was forgiven. 'L'Orange,' said Suleiman, as though he'd put something rancid in his mouth, 'has departed for his HQ in the depths of a Swiss mountain where, rumour has it, he not only stores his artworks in a massive temperature- and humidity-controlled vault, he also hangs from the cavern ceiling among thousands of chittering, blood-sucking bats who excrete sleet storms of guano and revere him as their god.'

Any biographer of l'Orange who scorns this deceptively throwaway remark will be scorned in turn by shrewder colleagues. It is, I suspect, bats and all, correct in every detail.

Likewise my deduction that the torch thief is one of l'Orange's shadowy agents, as well as an ailing former tennis pro, etc.

Which makes me wonder ... Why, given that the torch thief has almost certainly been ravaged by long-term drug abuse, and is chronically depressed because he's going to have to declare himself bankrupt, and is of confused sexuality despite his three wives and numerous deliriously snortaholic one-night stands with pole dancers, and has a banana bend to his abnormally long penis, and thinks his dour Christian Fundamentalist foster parents never really loved him (perhaps they were incapable of loving him, and perhaps for good reason, but perhaps it was just because of his left-handedness and westerly-inclined penis, which suggested a penis that was forever seeking its master's guiding hand, resulting inevitably, so they concluded, temptation being what it is and the flesh weak, so very, very weak, in Beelzebubish bouts of onanism) – why, despite all of those things, things that I somehow know to be true, or almost certainly true, can't I seem to narrow the gap between us? After all, he's on foot and I'm riding a pushbike, albeit a damaged one, and bikes, even ones as damaged as this, should confer a 10mph speed advantage over someone running.

It's a mystery. On which I had no time to dwell. In the distance I heard a faint, strangulated cry, borne to me on an obliging gust of wind. Simultaneously a flash of lightning shot across my field of vision. When my eyes readjusted, the firefly glow of the torch was nowhere to be seen, and without that distant beacon I was travelling blind. The night was pitch black, and the periodic shower of sparks, generated by the bike's front wheel scraping against the forks, illuminated nothing but itself. I rode much more slowly now, cautiously, in the secure knowledge that at any moment I could hit a kerb or traffic island and be sent sprawling. I was also aware that the canal was nearby. How? Any native of our fair city would know the answer to that question. Because I could smell the dilute discharge, urinous and reeking of rotting flesh, from the tannery on the city's industrial edge. Plunging into the canal would be inimical to health. Also, I'd never learned how to swim.

I slowed to a crawl and was coasting, standing on the pedals, trying in vain to see what lay ahead, when something struck me hard in the chest, flipping me over the back wheel and onto the road. This manoeuvre was accompanied by an explosion of light and what sounded, near at hand, like a giggle. As I crashed onto my back, head and shoulders first, time telescoped in on itself. In that frozen moment I assumed, because of the blinding flash, and because I couldn't move a muscle and was struggling for breath, that I'd broken my neck and would spend my remaining days as a quadriplegic, strapped into a motorised chair that I'd operate with my best eyelid, the blinks of the weaker eyelid providing my sole means of communication.

But what upset me most of all – even, bizarrely, more than the thought of being crippled for life – was that I'd lost sight of the torch, for in losing sight of it I'd managed to lose it completely. How would I, newly crippled, bat blind but without bat radar, cloaked in this oppressive, all-pervasive darkness, manage to find the torch again? It could be anywhere. And, for that matter, so could I.

I was lost, the torch was lost, and my name would go down in history as the person who lost it. The great loser: that's what they'd call me. Even the worst of my predecessors, the notorious celebrity chef who was so incapacitated by drink that he completed the run hours late, on all fours, crawling through pools of his own vomit, managed by some miracle (which, after spending several months in rehab, he attributed to the intervention of Martin and Monica, the his-and-hers patron saints of alcoholics, and their pal Bibiana, patron saint of hangovers) ... even he, drunk as a skunk, had managed to hold on to the torch, something I'd signally failed to do.

Songs that would have been written and sung in my honour, to my greater glory, songs of celebration, will now consist of jibes at my seemingly meticulous yet, in practice, comically inadequate preparations for the run. They'll broadcast to the whole world, in sarcastic verse and rabble-rousing chorus, that I'm a dolt, the knucklehead son of knucklehead parents, a family of knuckleheads, generation upon generation of us going back all the way to the ark where, presumably, we were boarded with the two-by-twos, ape class, rather than with Noah's kin. No doubt the songwriters, cynical opportunists that they are, heartless bastards one and all, will neglect to mention the nigh insuperable odds I faced: the vengeful former girlfriend; the ill-fitting costume she made that was calculated to rob me of dignity and easy mobility; the contemptible behaviour and gross negligence of the events committee; the thick cloud cover through which barely a glimmer of light could pass; and, to top it all, Charles 'Blood' l'Orange with his ugly voice, gangster demeanour and sinister machinations.

Yes, I made a mistake. A bad one. I took a wrong turn and got lost. Such things happen. But my intentions were good.

Unfortunately, as we all know, outcomes are what count, not intentions, otherwise we'd be living in a state of Utopian bliss rather than in grey, post-industrial cities such as this, nursing our grievances and grumbling about ... well, everything.

⊖

As I mused bitterly on my fall from grace, I began to feel a tingle in the fingers of my left hand, then an irritating tickle on the opposing wrist, both so slight they might well be figments of my imagination, the equivalent of phantom limb pain. Within three or four minutes, sensation returned to every part of my body and I was once again in agony. I struggled to my feet and took a tentative step, thinking to retrieve the bicycle from where it had fallen. Something caught at my throat and lightning flashed. Dazzled, I staggered back, and in bringing a hand up to my throat I snagged the thing that had touched me. Lightning flashed again. What I'd encountered, I realised, was a wire strung tautly across the road. Every time I touched it there was an explosion of light. Resting my fingertips gently on the wire, I tracked along it to where a flashgun was strapped to a lamp post with duct tape. Beside the post was a tripod, minus camera.

My fingers were wet, and when I sniffed them I knew the wetness was blood – not mine, the blood of the torch thief who'd run full tilt into l'Orange's trap. But where was he now? Where, for that matter, was bully boy l'Orange himself?

I peeled away the tape, freeing the flashgun and its battery pack. Pointing the gun away from me, I triggered the flash once, twice, three times, in a ninety-degree sweep. By the third flash my eyes were better adjusted and I was able to identify where I was – Proud Street, a name that could hardly be less fitting. This was the crooked, pot-holed main thoroughfare through Larkspur, the city's poorest suburb, a dangerous place, part slum, part demolished, inhabited by thieves and scoundrels in unhappily close quarter with their victims – the destitute, the homeless, the drug addicted and alcoholic, the abused, the brain-fried, the weak, lame and halt. It was where people ended up when there was nowhere else for them to go. It was where they came to suffer and die. The city's tourist information website carefully avoided all mention of Larkspur, and the route I was meant to follow had carefully skirted its ragged northern fringe. But perhaps l'Orange had battered the events committee into submission by the hurricane force of his will, and the route on which I found myself had been re-designated as the official one. Perhaps I hadn't strayed at all.

What the flashgun also revealed was my bicycle, which, now that I could see it, seemed to be in terrible condition, so ramshackle that no-one in Larkspur would deign to steal it. I decided to leave the bike where it lay, its front wheel wedged under a burnt-out vehicle like a piglet trying to suckle at a dead sow's teat.

A few yards off to the left, something that looked like a running shoe was sticking at an odd angle out of a monstrous privet hedge. As I approached it, I flashed the gun again, illuminating the hedge interior. The man lay upside down, caught fast among the lower branches, his head and shoulders twisted towards me. Even in that brief flash of light, I could see the nasty wound to his neck where he'd run into the wire prior to being thrown (I assume – how else could he have got there?) into the hedge. He seemed to be unconscious. Or was feigning it. I knew at a glance he wasn't my understudy because he was dressed in streetwear: dark grey hoodie top, badly faded black tracksuit bottoms; no official ill-fitting costume, no winged helmet. Regrettably, there was also no sign of the torch he'd taken from me.

I leaned deep into the hedge and shook him roughly by the shoulder. 'Hoy! Wake up! Where's the torch? Who did this to you?'

His response came so fast I hadn't quite finished speaking:

'Fuck off! Leave me alone, you shitty piece of shit! You shit-faced fucking cunt bastard!' The wire had obviously damaged his larynx, his voice was a croak. I could barely make out what he was saying. 'Fuck off! Fuck off and die! Just fucking fuck off, okay!' Then, in sorrow: 'My wife'll fucking kill me when she hears about this. You have no idea what I have to put up with, not a fucking clue.'

My sympathies were entirely with the wife. But this was Larkspur, after all; each was probably as bad as the other.

In a tone of voice that oozed sweet reason, I said, 'Listen, here's the deal. If you tell me who waylaid you and took the torch, I'll pull you out of the hedge. And if you know where the torch has been taken, and you help me get it back, I'll make a hero of you. I won't mention the fact that you ambushed me. I'll say you were the good samaritan who sprang from nowhere in my hour of need and stood by me. I'll say that without your help the torch wouldn't have been recovered, and consequently, for the first time in its seven-hundred-year history (plague years notwith-standing), the annual run would've had to be abandoned. More than just a hero, you'll be deemed a prince among men, a secular saint. In gratitude, the mayor will bestow the freedom of the city on you and the police will be encouraged to lose your casework file.'

Okay, lay it on thick, but make it sound plausible.

'Women, beautiful women, will want to sleep with you without first asking for money; they'll be hoping to get impregnated and have your babies. And that's not all. To express their gratitude and gain valuable publicity, manufacturers and retailers will shower you with consumer goods – fridges, TVs, cars, bedroom suites, laptops, golf clubs, loft insulation, boxer shorts, you name it. Our city's top university, respected worldwide, will offer you an honorary degree, perhaps in applied criminology.'

Now crank it up a bit, steady as you go.

'But wait, that's not all. You'll be interviewed by the national press, and with the help of a PR guru, someone like Max Clifford, or perhaps Max Clifford himself if he's no longer in jail –'

'Or dead.'

'Or, as you say, dead ... you'll become an A-list celebrity, attending movie premieres with the likes of Emily Watson and Keeley Hawes, Helena Bonham Carter and Helen Mirren. At one such premiere, while squiring one or more of these alluring women on the red carpet, you're sure to bump into George Clooney, who as a staunch advocate of social justice will be fascinated by the way you've turned your life around. And he's a generous chap, as everyone knows. After a discreet word from your guru, it's odds on that he'll invite you to spend quality time with him and his lovely wife Amal at their magnificent residence on Lake Como.'

More, more, rising to dizzy heights.

'Having got to know and respect you, George will be keen to buy the film rights to your unwritten auto-biography and assume the lead role – you – himself. You are, after all, very much alike. Getting wind of this via your guru, rival publishers will enter into a frenzied bidding war, offering astronomical sums of money for your life story, which will then be ghost written in little more than a fortnight by a functioning alcoholic ex-hack. In gritty prose, pulling no punches, it will describe your tough upbringing in slumland and how, in the hormonal throes of adolescence, having discovered the heady joys of poetry, you decided you didn't want to follow in your father's footsteps and become an enforcer for the Krays or the Richardsons or some other notorious crime family because –'

'Krays.'

'Say again.'

'The Krays. Granddad was one of their accountants. Not a turf accountant, either, mind you, a proper one. Ronnie Kray used to dandle dad on his knee when he was little, so I've been told.'

No swearing. Perhaps I was getting somewhere.

'So do we have a deal? Will you help me find the torch?'

'Of course I fucking won't, dick brain. Now fuck off and leave me in peace.'

'You don't want me to pull you out of the hedge?'

'No.'

'Why not?'

'Because I'm *busy*, that's why – *meditating*. I'm a Buddhist. Not that it's any of your fucking business.'

What to do, what to do. Time is ticking by. The longer this takes, the farther away l'Orange and the torch will be. Gripping the running shoe firmly in both hands, I start to twist his foot clockwise using all the strength I can muster.

'Ow!' he says, but without much conviction.

Bracing myself and putting all my weight into it, I twist harder, then harder still. I can feel the strain in my shoulders, the muscles tightening across my back. Torture is something new to me, new and unappealing. But needs must. Presumably, if I don't start to enjoy it, all will be well. Grunting and gasping with the exertion, I use every ounce of my not inconsiderable strength to twist his foot, pushing it fractionally further out of true with every word I utter:

'Where *[gasp]* is *[grunt]* the *[gasp]* torch?'

'Ow!' he says. 'Ow! – Ow! – Ow!' And then I know I've got him. There's a sob, a croaky sob. It's the most pitiful sound I've ever heard, and I feel truly ashamed. But all qualms must be set aside. It's too late to stop now. Taking a deep breath, and to a mounting crescendo of sobs, I force his foot over to the three o'clock position. Then just a bit further. And then a bit too far. With a loud crack, his foot spins round and ends up facing completely the wrong way. My gorge rises when I realise what I've done. This is terrible. But then I realise something even more terrible ... those croaky sobs are actually croaky laughs. The torch thief is laughing. I've broken his foot, snapped it at the ankle, shattered a host of smaller bones in the process and torn various ligaments, and he's laughing about it, a horrible, croaky laugh that will permeate my dreams and sour even the sweetest of them for years to come.

⊖

Things then get a little confused. I find myself cradling the foot, the poor, sickly thing. I'm caressing it as though it were a fretful infant in need of a lullaby. Right on cue, my throat aching with tenderness, I start to croon: *Little foot, little foot, sleep in your shoe / sleep for a spell and all will be well.* Sudden tears scald my cheeks. Just as I'm about to plant a kiss on the toecap, my emotions begin to fluctuate wildly. In a spasm of revulsion so violent it feels like I'm being turned inside out, I uncradle the foot as though it were suddenly red hot. There's every reason to believe it will stay where it is, hanging limply at the end of the leg of a man upended in a hedge. Instead it slips through my fingers and lands on my toes. As one, the torch thief and I go 'Ow!' But in tone our exclamations could hardly be more different. Mine is of pain and astonishment. In his I detect nothing but mockery.

I trigger the flashgun. The running shoe lies on its side in the gutter. Twisted metal, a shattered joint and torn flesh-coloured plastic jut from the heel – the mangled remains of a prosthetic limb.

The croaky laughter starts up again.

What to do, what to do.

Out of the corner of my eye, in the distance, I see the hearse crossing the top of Proud Street, where Larkspur borders Sheepwash. The hearse moves at such a funereal pace it appears to be standing still. The coffin section is softly illuminated, flouting the lighting ban; the driver's cab is bathed in official darkness. I'm worn to a frazzle. My body aches all over, as though I'd been beaten with a length of rubber hose. Nothing would please me more than to clamber into the coffin's soft satin interior, bask in that sepulchral glow, and sleep, sleep, sleep ...

But no matter how weary I am or how weary I become, I've got to catch up with the hearse, and soon. May it offer sweet salvation.

Ignoring the torch thief's foul, histrionic croaks – 'Help me, you tampon-chomping bastard! You shit on a stick! Help me! Don't be such a spunkface, you useless streak of frozen piss. Where the fuck is your humanity? Help me!' – I set off at a stagger and graduate to a stumbling run.

2. The Eternal

> On your last day on Earth
> The sun rises like on any other
> But when night falls
> It lasts forever
> > – Anon

How I completed the run was unorthodox, to say the least. Using the flashgun to guide my way along Proud Street, I gained my second wind just as the battery started to fade. Curiously, the pain caused by the ill-fitting costume didn't hamper me now, it registered hardly at all. I flew along as though the wings on my helmet and ankles were as powerful as jet engines.

When a mugger lunged from a side street and tried to grapple with me, I thrust the depleted flashgun into his hands and swerved nimbly round him without losing pace. During my days on the Tennis Federation's pro circuit I was known as a baseline slammer, my matches won almost exclusively on serve alone. What power and skill I had were vested in my upper body rather than my legs. Who then would have thought me capable of such fancy footwork? But things were different now. I reached the hearse in three giant strides. Slapping a hand on the vehicle's glossy rump to alert the driver to my presence, I tripped and sprawled on the tarmac. My understudy, whom I hadn't noticed and in truth had forgotten about, crashed into my legs. He landed on me like a hod of bricks.

Once again, Mr Suleiman picked me up, but instead of lowering me gently onto a chaise longue, as before, he placed me in my coffin and folded my arms across my chest. The coffin was every bit as plush and well appointed as I'd hoped it would be. A snug fit, too. 'Moth to the flame,' he said, a little sadly. Having checked for signs of life, the hearse medic switched off the light in the coffin section, and he and Mr Suleiman returned to the cab. There was a long silence before either of them spoke. Much of what they said was masked by the glass partition that separated us and the engine's feline purr, but this is what I heard:

Suleiman: 'I told them it was a mistake, but would they listen? ... Wrong man for the job, I said. Even worse than the sozzled chef of yesteryear, though at least he brought corporate sponsorship with him ... Well, what's done is done. Better send Zeitgeister ahead with the spare torch, he's in full costume and knows the route inside out.'

Is that my understudy's name? Zeitgeister? Never heard of him, on court or off.

Medic: 'What about l'Orange? He and his little gang are hereabouts, skulking in the shadows.'

No, I definitely don't recall a Zeitgeister on the pro circuit, not in my time.

Suleiman: 'As a champion cage fighter, believe me, Zeitgeister can look after himself ... But he'll meet his match in l'Orange, that malevolent, obnoxious bastard with his arty, UDA-derived guerrilla tactics.'

With that we set off. The hearse's soothing engine note, its cosseting suspension, and the sheer sumptuousness of the coffin's satin-lined upholstery, conspired to lull me into a kind of sleep that wasn't quite sleep, in that I was relaxed and rested but fully conscious throughout. Quite frankly, I'd never felt better, but perhaps that's because I wasn't feeling very much at all.

⊖

We passed uneventfully through Sheepwash, then started on the tortuous climb through Framley's maze of narrow streets. This was the part of the run I'd always found most challenging. Not just because of the steepness of the hill, 1:4 mostly, but also because of the disorientating switchbacks and numerous unsignposted dead ends. Even in first gear the hearse struggled on the steeper sections, and some of the corners were so tight they had to be taken as three-point turns, involving hard revving and occasional clutch slippage. Apparently, Zeitgeister was as agile as a mountain goat and kept to schedule with the precision of an atomic clock, whereas the hearse occasionally fell behind and, to Mr Suleiman's consternation, Zeitgeister disappeared for several minutes at a time.

All credit to Mr Suleiman, he really did care what happened to Zeitgeister. And to me, too, despite his earlier harsh criticism. Was I stung by what he said? Oddly, no. Which should have surprised me. But I had entered into a state of such profound relaxation that my emotions were ... is quiescent the right word? Disengaged? Whichever: I was incapable of being surprised, and it troubled me not a jot. I felt that nothing would ruffle my feathers ever again.

Nor did it, not even when l'Orange's black-clad militia launched an attack on the hearse.

They came whooping down from the hills like Sioux braves in a classic American horse opera, their ranks swollen by (so I imagined) tattooed mercenaries, knuckle-draggers sprung from the depths of the criminal underworld. Or perhaps, given that we were approaching the municipal graveyard, from Hades itself.

We had just struggled round a tricky u-bend on

Alexander Cummings Street, a manoeuvre that delayed us by several minutes. The long uphill stretch to Cemetery Rise lay ahead. Zeitgeister should have been no more than thirty metres away, running on the spot as per instructions until the hearse caught up with him, but he and the torch were nowhere to be seen.

'No,' groaned Mr Suleiman. 'Please, no.' That was the last I heard from him.

The l'Orangeans struck the hearse with the force of an avalanche, buffeting it in waves, rocking the vehicle violently from side to side and almost overturning it. Mr Suleiman and the medic were pulled from the cab, then trussed, gagged and carted off in the direction of the graveyard. 'Caw! Caw! Caw! Caw!' cried their captors as they whisked them away.

Only then did I realise who we were dealing with.

It was the battle cry of the Revolutionary Undertakers, so-called, a group principally known for disrupting showbiz funerals. This was not a frivolous pursuit. On environmental grounds they were staunch advocates of sky burial, as practised in Tibet according to Buddhist tradition. Their aim was to establish a charnel ground in the Peak District, where birds and other animals could gradually strip flesh from the bones of the dead. A natural process, ecologically sound.

But although several all-party early day motions on this issue were submitted to the House of Commons by sympathetic MPs, and the EDMs acquired a large number of signatures from fellow MPs throughout the Midlands and Northern England, no debate ensued. Nor, they were told, was it ever likely to. Adding insult to injury, for five consecutive years the BIFD (British Institute of Funeral Directors) refused to allow the matter to be discussed at their annual conference, not even in closed session, deeming it 'in rather poor taste' and 'too cranky for our core clientele'. This I knew from the grumbles of a master stonemason whose yard lay opposite my flat.

Frustrated by the lack of progress, a dozen of the more hardline sky burialists donned black ski masks and founded a provisional wing to further the cause by direct action. Sending trained crows to harry both the official mourners and the zombie army of gawpers at showbiz funerals became their favoured tactic. The crows swooped down in full confrontation mode, gleefully plucking off hats and toupees, tearing apart the floral displays, defecating copiously on one and all, and driving them with wing, beak and claw from the grave site. Then, as calm as you please, they perched photogenically on the abandoned coffin by the open grave. After a handful of striking photos had been electronically despatched to newspapers worldwide, the crows and their handlers scattered among the tombstones and up into the clouds.

Although I had nothing to do with showbiz and wasn't a celebrity – except by dint of what I'd been asked to do and, to my regret, had utterly failed to do – it was obvious that disrupting the run would provide the Revolutionary Undertakers with banner headlines. And despite the fact that the RU provos had almost nothing in common with l'Orange, it was assumed by those in the know that a collaboration of sorts was, at some point, inevitable. Mr Suleiman had said as much, had in fact written several memos to that effect, but, as he told the hearse medic, the events committee paid no heed. Yet another example of their gross negligence.

One of the undertakers tried to close my eyelids and rotate my lower jaw. I felt nothing, no sensation at all. 'Stiffening up nicely, I'd say,' he said. 'Well advanced, in fact.' From somewhere behind him a voice called out, 'Rigor's begun, Mr Orange. He's almost ready.'

'Right,' said the first undertaker. 'On a count of three, shoulder the casket.'

'Coffin,' someone shot back.

'Don't be such a pedant, Jim,' sighed a third. 'It gets tiresome after a while.'

'Look, it's six-sided, not four. It's anthropoid in shape. By my reckoning, and I've spent nearly thirty years in this business, man and boy, that makes it a coffin. Not, most definitely not, a casket. These things matter. If we don't use the correct terms we'll –'

'Whoa, Jim, it was a slip of the tongue. A mere slip of the tongue. No need to get all worked up about it.'

'Lads,' chipped in a fourth, the conciliator, 'let's discuss it later, eh, over a pint. We've got more important things to do right now.'

Grunts of acknowledgement and approval.

'One, two and uh – *three.*'

I was hoisted, feather light, or so they made it seem, onto the shoulders of four very strong men, pallbearing titans, exemplars of the funeral directors' trade.

'On three, best foot forward. One, two and uh –'

⊖

Eight stages of the run had yet to be completed, touching on all of the city's remaining suburbs. The order of transit: Uppersalt, Mount Pleasant, Cinderhill, Lower Hedgley, Beulah Bottom, Staups Carr, Bezzum and Daisy Parade, bypassing the new executive housing developments of Cheney Oaks and Trinity Elms, both of which hid behind electronically controlled security gates and consisted of nothing but treeless cul-de-sacs. The runner would by then have looped back to the heart of the city. If all went according to plan, he would reach the Bank Street terminus, by the town hall steps, just as the sun emerged from behind the eastern hills ...

A local hero!

Bringer of light and good fortune!

The city could now breathe easy. It would thrive for yet another year and he, the runner, with it.

⊖

But in my case that's not what happened.

⊖

While the undertakers huffed and puffed up the hill, I took a moment to review the situation. The wind had died down and the clouds were starting to disperse. Through the rectangular viewing window in the lid of the coffin, twinkling stars could occasionally be seen. I knew my muscles must be stiffening up, but in such a confined space I had no way of flexing them. Not that I could actually feel any stiffness. Nor aches. Nor pains. Even my probably broken nose had stopped throbbing.

As I'm sure you can imagine, the ride on the undertakers' shoulders was not as smooth as that of the hearse, but their lock-step speed-walker march, honed to perfection by years of diligent practice, had its own lulling rhythm. Although the lid of the coffin had been fastened down, and external sounds were muffled, the lead undertaker's head was right next to mine, separated by only two centimetres of wood. I could hear him issuing commands and providing his colleagues with information as to the hazards that lay ahead. 'Slight dip,' he said, sotto voce, 'fifteen paces, followed by a 12° turn to the left achievable in ten paces, starting … hang on, almost there … *now*!' And: 'Speed bumps ahead. Only a damn fool would situate them near a graveyard. Hearses should glide like swans on still water, not look as though they're running a steeplechase. Be that as it may, bumps, two sets, some thirty-five paces apart, the first set coming up ten paces from ... *now.*' That sort of thing.

I'd thought my breath, however negligible, would fog the viewing window within a minute or two, but that hadn't happened. The stars juddered and twinkled, perfectly plain. Dark clouds slid by. The moon was resting out of sight. 'Uppersalt straight ahead,' I heard. 'Good work, lads. Sixty more paces, gradually slowing, starting ... *now.*' Clomp, clomp, clomp, clomp. 'Right,' he said, when we came to a halt, 'let's take a breather while l'Orange's lot do their bit.'

The bit that l'Orange's lot did consisted of leaning my coffin against a local landmark, or in close proximity to a street sign, opening the lid fully and wedging the shaft of the torch into an almost invisible perspex frame that was clamped to my left arm. The frame gave the impression that I was both cradling the torch and bearing it aloft. Dozens of photos were then taken. Apart from the chattering of camera shutters, this was all done silently, without noticeable instruction from l'Orange. The synchronised flashgun bursts were dazzling, but as I didn't blink I didn't spoil a single shot.

At Uppersalt there was almost a mishap. When the l'Orangeans propped up the coffin, I wasn't quite as stiff as they thought I would be. I slumped badly and bent forward at the waist, almost toppling onto the road. A hook of some kind was hastily found and screwed into the base of the coffin, at head height, and the neckline of my official costume was attached to it, to keep me, torch and all, standing erect. But by the time we reached Cinderhill the hook was no longer needed. One of the black-clad militiamen declared, 'Better posture now, Mr Orange,' eliciting by way of response an unfathomable growl.

Photos were taken at every key stage in each of the suburbs en route to the terminus. The streets remained empty. Not even a stray cat crossed our path. The much-vaunted urban-camouflaged medics, who were, according to Mr Suleiman, ready to dash to my aid with bandages, splints, salves and a vast pharmacopeia of pick-me-ups, were notable by their absence. As they had been throughout the run. Not that I needed aid, as far as I could tell, not now ... But earlier, well, that was a different matter.

I said a few minutes ago that I'd reviewed the situation. But self-reflection wasn't my strongest suit, and things external to me were, or had always seemed, slightly beyond my control. As a child I'd daydreamed endlessly and walked in my sleep, ate in my sleep, read books in my sleep (and, to everyone's surprise, could recall them perfectly, line by line, the following day). I went out into the world in the middle of the night and walked around, climbed church spires, broke into banks and other supposedly secure buildings, and once even swam across a flood-swollen river during a winter storm. All in my sleep.

Sometimes I was found dozens of miles from home. On one occasion I was taken in, footsore and weary, by Romany travellers, who fed me and taught me how to play cards, insisting that I should learn such things because I had 'the ultimate poker face'. They were right: I won every hand, even when, in desperation, they cheated with a marked deck.

To keep me at home overnight, mother barred and locked all the windows and doors, locked the keys in a squat fire- and earthquake-proof safe that was bolted to the cellar floor, and hid the safe key about her person in what she called 'Mummy's secret place'. Being small for my age and slight of build, I escaped via the chimney. That was the last straw. She took me to a specialist who immediately referred us to other specialists who subjected me to myriad tests. Years of them. The treatment changed according to the diagnosis and the diagnosis was as changeable as the weather. Although no effort was spared, no cure was found. But one day I snapped out of it and never snapped in again. My daydreams became night dreams and occasionally nightmares. Suddenly I was, for want of a better word, normal.

And normal I remain to this day, whereas the world and everything in it has behaved more and more abnormally, changing by increments so small they usually pass unnoticed and even when noticed prove very hard to reconcile. The ability to control events and circumstances is often beyond me, and even the few things I manage to grasp soon slip through my fingers.

For example, on a particularly fine September morning giving promise of dazzle and bliss, I received a letter which, without explanation, stated that I was the presumptive nominee in a contest without peer, 'the chosen one', and should await further instructions. Naturally, I thought it the work of a crank, or some kind of scam. But barely half an hour later, representatives of Citywide Arts arrived and had me sign a sheaf of official-looking documents. They were as polite as Jehovah's Witnesses – which, at first, is what I took them to be – but extremely assertive, brooking no argument. No-one asked whether I wished to do the solstice run, it was just assumed that not only would I agree to it, if asked, thereby eliminating the need to be asked, I'd consider it an honour. My attempts to raise doubts and broach legitimate concerns were shushed. The honour proved impossible to decline: a fait accompli.

As one, and without prior indication of intent, the Citywide Arts representatives stood up, just as the daily newspaper was delivered. One of the reps, a thuggish-looking Buddha in a business suit, retrieved it from the welcome mat, folded it neatly, face up, and with a short bow placed it solemnly in my hands as though performing a ritual as old as time whose meaning has long been forgotten. But at a glance I recognised the gravity of the situation. The lead article bore a picture of me in my heyday striking a tennis ball with considerable force. To all intents and purposes my fate was sealed.

⊖

Since then, things had got steadily worse. I'd been, in

no particular order, mugged, humiliated, kidnapped, abandoned and, quite possibly, killed (I still wasn't entirely sure of my status). We were now approaching Beulah Bottom, on the downhill stretch, wending our way back to the heart of the city. The undertakers, aided by gravity, were finding the going much easier, but even so the run was arduous, the pace swift, and I could tell they were utterly exhausted because, above the ragged sound of their panting, the lead undertaker's voice sounded strained and his navigational advice was stripped to the bone.

'Roundabout,' he said. *[pant, pant]* 'Second exit.' *[pant, pant]* 'No countdown, lads.' *[pant, pant]* 'Follow my lead.'

They did as he said and all went well until we reached a notorious blackspot near Staups Carr, a hard left on greasy cobblestones with a treacherous adverse camber, known to locals as The Wall of Death. The coffin's rear end slewed round when one of the tailgaters lost his footing and kicked the legs out from under his partner. As they fell, bringing the others down with them, the coffin hit the road with a resounding crash that dislodged my dental plate and wedged it in the back of my throat. Feet first, the coffin slithered away from the fallen undertakers. By the time it left the road it had gained considerable momentum, enough to carry it down a short grassy slope and into Brindle Pond, scattering sleepy wildfowl to the four winds. Amid the birds' indignant squawks and panicked flight, I heard men shouting and scrabbling in my wake. The coffin drifted serenely out into the centre of the pond, as watertight and shipshape as I knew it would be: a noble craft, a vessel fit for a hero – which is what I was, I suppose, even if only by default.

Certainly, like all heroes, I have my flaws, forgetfulness being one of them. In my last will and testament, hurriedly drawn up by the legal services division of Citywide Arts on the day before the run, I'd failed to stipulate that if the worse came to the worst I wanted to receive a Viking-style longboat funeral. Such a stipulation had been written into my mother's will, and my father's before her, and had been honoured in token fashion. Their coffins, though of regular size, had been shaped like Viking longboats, and their graves were mounded higher than usual: mini-tumuli. But I'd long hankered after something more than just a symbolic representation of our Viking heritage.

To think that being cast adrift on a scummy urban pond should remind me of this.

⊖

When we were together again on dry land, the run continued. But the end, as apocalyptophiles joyfully proclaim, was nigh. I was in a daze of reminiscence unparalleled in my hitherto unreflective life, and I hardly noticed the wild cheers of the Bank Street crowd. Nor the moment when the cheers began to fade as they realised that this year's solstice runner was completing the run in a coffin. Was it a cheap stunt? Someone evidently thought so. 'Shame!' he cried. Others began to jostle their neighbours and argue the toss. There were boos and catcalls, revealing deep hostility and the threat of mob violence. Bathed in pale illumination meant to emulate moonlight, the mayor, his lady wife, their children, and various civic dignitaries stood on a platform overlooking the crowd. Mr Suleiman had talked me through the programme of events several weeks earlier, so I knew what to expect. The mayor would step to the microphone, give a short, cliché-ridden speech that no-one cared a damn about, and shake my hand. With as much sincerity as I could muster, I was to say two words and two words only: *Thank you.* Loud applause. Cue martial music (an orchestral salute with brass section blare and kettle drum roar). Then, in the hush that followed, and at the precise moment the sun rose above the hills, the torch would be doused in a glowing golden bowl. Deafening applause, birdlike shrieks, monkey house whoops and hollers!

But, apparently, the sight of my coffin completely flummoxed the mayor. He said nothing and stood stock still. The police, exercising an unusual degree of restraint, or perhaps stricken by the same indecision that had stricken the mayor, did nothing. Only the undertakers seemed to know what to do. They plunged into the heart of the crowd like an icebreaker sundering an Arctic floe. Their destination: the General Hospital's A&E department, a block further on, where, having laid me down on the unattended reception desk, they sprinted outdoors into the burgeoning dawn and went their several ways – 'Caw! Caw! Caw! Caw!'

Almost immediately, a man with two black eyes and a torn eyebrow peered in at me through the coffin's viewing window. What he saw was clearly not to his liking, for he ran to fetch a doctor, eventually finding one in the staff canteen still chewing his breakfast oats. The doctor removed the coffin lid, checked my pulse at wrist and neck, placed the metal bell of his stethoscope on the ribs over my heart, shone a bright light into one eye then the other (I didn't blink on either occasion) and, noticing my displaced denture, hooked it with a salty forefinger from where it had lodged in my windpipe. Porters were instructed to take me to Rose Cottage, which lacked roses and wasn't by any stretch of the imagination a cottage. It was the mortuary, a windowless concrete bunker. 'Use the shrubbery path,' he said, 'round the back of the building. And duck below the windows when you pass those poor devils in the hospice ward. Even at this early hour, some of them will be awake and contemplating their imminent demise.'

At Rose Cottage, men in identical smocks lifted me from my coffin, stripped me naked, covered me from head to toe with a plain grey sheet and slid me feet first into a drawer of the largest filing cabinet I'd ever seen.

⊖

No sooner had they done so than the drawer slid open and the sheet was folded down to my chest. Same smocks, different men. A different day, too. According to a clock situated high on the wall it was 11:47, 22 December, the day after I'd completed the run. Days were turning into minutes, hours into seconds; time was collapsing in on itself. I'd experienced this kind of thing before, during my post-tennis years of alcohol abuse and dogged sensory derangement. Once I'd stayed awake for five days and five nights, drinking alone, curtains closed, phone off the hook, and all I could recall of that one-hundred-and-twenty-hour binge was that at some point, whether day or night I couldn't say, it rained heavily, drumming on the roof like a thousand dancing imps in cleated wooden clogs, and, however improbably, the rain smelled of strawberries.

Mr Suleiman's face loomed large above mine. 'Yes,' he said with a sigh, 'that's our boy.' And, ambiguously: 'If only our resident astrologer had predicted this.'

He stepped back and my partially sighted neighbour, Henry, took his place. I had no next of kin, so Mr Suleiman had been made the executor of my will and Henry was the sole beneficiary. Because the things he'd inherit were worthless – tacky knick-knacks, broken (in frustration) tennis racquets, skip furniture and the like – I knew he'd have to pay someone to dispose of them. I'd made a bequest to a local house clearance firm to cover that eventuality.

Henry's fingertips ran like rivulets from my hairline to my chin, then he kneaded my face like putty. 'Oh my,' he said in dismay. 'The nose is much flatter. I think it's broken. Gravel is embedded in his chin and large clumps of beard are missing. But it's him all right; the transverse hairs in those caterpillar eyebrows I'd recognise anywhere.'

One of the smockmen stripped the sheet from me with a stage magician's flourish, and the other, playing the part of his glamorous assistant, hip-swayed and chasséd as he folded it neatly in squares and took it away. Then a man in a full surgical gown, mob cap and face mask began to pore over every inch of my body with an illuminated magnifying glass. What he was looking for, I had no idea. 'Turn him over, gentlemen, if you please,' he said, and they did. And when he had finished: 'That's that, then. Hose him down.'

Where had Henry and Mr Suleiman got to? One minute they were there, next minute gone. Whenever my concentration lapsed a chunk of time disappeared, and distracting thoughts kept coming, unbidden, unstoppable.

Meanwhile, the man in the surgical gown had been joined by a taller man, similarly attired. I tried to pay close attention to what they were doing to me, but my thoughts kept straying. My mind seemed to have a mind of its own. I wondered, for example, what had

happened to Mr Suleiman and the medic and, presumably, Zeitgeister when they were carted off to the
graveyard by the Revolutionary Undertakers. Zeitgeister had, I felt sure, been brought down by a tran-
quiliser dart, the kind used on big cats in the Maasai
Mara. No doubt the three of them were then locked
up in one of the many ostentatious tombs, big as a
house, that held the mortal remains of Victorian cap-
tains of industry and their kin.

'So this is our runner, is it?' said the taller man.
'Poor sod, look at the state of him. I gather he was a
racquet player of distinction in his day. Badminton, I
think. Not a sport I follow.'

'Well, his day is done,' said the other man, 'and
this' – he withdrew my heart, slick with blood, from
the wet, sucking cavity in my chest – 'is why.'

'Open it up, then. Let's see the damage.'

'Whoa, hold hard! An athlete – massive exertion –
additional stress – sudden death. We both know what
that suggests: an artery anomaly of some kind. Even a
typically knuckle-brained first-year med student
could work that one out. Let's try to be more precise
and make it interesting, shall we? Fifty quid says it's
an acute angle take-off and kinking of the coronary
artery as it arises from the aorta.'

'Okay, you're on. Fifty it is. But in my opinion the
cause of death is more likely to be a flap-like closure
of the abnormal slit-like coronary orifice, and my
opinion is based on a wealth of knowledge and experience, a veritable Taj Mahal of it, whereas your

knowledge is, by comparison, meagre, the equivalent of a dilapidated turf hut. And let's not speak of your experience, not without yielding a seismic shudder, given that the few patients who've managed to survive your ministrations are in the process of suing you, as are the families of those you've accidentally killed.'

Such raillery!

'You're an insufferable old goat, Jamieson, full of scalding piss and toxic wind, and when you were younger you were, if anything, even more insufferable than you are now, hard though that is to believe. I dearly wish you hadn't married my sister.'

'Agreed.'

They shook hands across my chest, and the tall one looked down at me with a twinkle in his eye and said, 'Sorry, chum. No disrespect intended. Life must go on, etc., and we should all do our best to enjoy it while we can.'

My heart was taken to a stainless steel table boasting flexible taps, sluices and a drain. A tray of sharp-tongued instruments was drawn alongside. The dissection took no time at all, three cuts of the scalpel.

'There, I told you so,' said the shorter fellow – or was it the tall one, Jamieson? They'd moved out of my line of sight and the timbre of their voices was similar, making it hard to tell them apart. 'That's a big fat bullseye you owe me.'

'Double or quits? The weight of his liver, to the nearest gram?'

'I don't see why not. Stuffing my wallet with your hard-earned cash is one of life's delicious little perks.'

One by one, my internal organs were removed, weighed, scrutinised and discarded. Notes were dictated into a voice-activated recorder. When they spoke it whirred, when they were silent it stopped. My mind did something similar. I tried hard to focus on what they were saying and doing, to hold on to reality and stop my thoughts from fragmenting. In vain. The bull mosquito whine of the bone saw, and the dip in pitch as the blade's jagged teeth bit into my skull, made it hard to concentrate. It reminded me of how my father used to remove the top of a soft-boiled egg with a circular scissor-like implement prior to dipping soldiers of buttered toast into the still runny yolk. And once, pausing momentarily, a laden soldier suspended between eggshell and mouth, he informed me that the Chinese (Vietnamese? Burmese? Sudanese? Japanese? Congolese? Portuguese? Singhalese? Balinese? Maltese? – he wasn't sure which) were rumoured to eat, as a delicacy, the brains of live monkeys.

That was one indignity this particular monkey wouldn't have to suffer.

Having made a complete circuit of my head with the bone saw, Jamieson removed the top of my skull with a quick twist, as though it were the lid of a vacuum-sealed jar, and placed it carefully, upside down, by my left ear. Before I knew what was happening, my brain had been removed and was being inspected.

He hummed and hawed and clicked his tongue several times before declaring it, all things considered, a surprisingly good specimen, apart from some small but significant lesions on the orbitofrontal cortex. 'Nancy,' he said into the voice recorder, for the benefit of the transcriber, 'italicise the bit about the lesions but cut out the banter and the gambling and anything that could be misconstrued by those of an uncharitable nature as unprofessional and/or insensitive, there's a dear. And this instruction too, of course.'

'I think we can safely say,' said the other man, 'that our runner's impulsive behaviour –'

'Contextually inappropriate –'

'Quite.'

'– poorly planned –'

'Yes.'

'– acted upon prematurely –'

'Couldn't agree more. You're on fire, Jamieson. I only wish that were literally the case.'

'– has on this occasion –'

'– On many previous occasions too, I shouldn't wonder –'

'– resulted in consequences decidedly adverse.'

'In this case, failure to complete the solstice run.'

'And something more. Of greater importance.'

'Of the greatest importance, I should say.'

'Indeed.'

'Yes indeed.'

'Death.'

Ah yes. Death. A notorious conversation stopper. But not here, not now. These were men who'd looked it squarely in the eye on numerous occasions and were undaunted by its basilisk gaze.

'And all because of a few little lesions,' said one (wistfully, I thought, but what do I know).

'Yes indeed,' said the other.

They each took a moment to savour their wisdom and compare it with that of their wanting colleague.

'I have it on good authority,' said Jamieson, 'and I mean *very* good authority, that during an aborted photo shoot with Charles l'Orange our runner kissed the artist full on the mouth and began to speak, as it were, in tongues.'

'Is that true?'

'As I say, *very* good authority. Tongues. Copious amounts of fluid would doubtless have been exchanged.'

'That ticks the impulsiveness box. But adverse consequences?'

'We should check for rabies.'

'*Rabies ...!*'

'For God's sake, Danvers, have you been living on Mars! Speculation about l'Orange is rife. From the arts pages to the sports section, the newspapers never tire of him – gossip mainly, and fabulous spin, the latter emanating from his crack PR team. He's reputed to live with ten thousand diseased bats in the most superbly outfitted cave – cavern, rather – in all of Switzerland. It's an immense bat hospice. He's

either the Mother Teresa of bats or St Francis incar-
nate. He comforts them as they near death and prepares them, as best he can, to meet their maker.'

'A full toxicology report?'

'And a psychiatric report, were it within our power
to request one. Both for l'Orange and this poor mutt.'

The mutt in question spent what seemed like
aeons examining this thought, turning it over in his
mind, all the while gazing at the ceiling tiles, cream,
square, perforated in a grid pattern, interspersed at
regular intervals with harsh strip lighting. He looked
without really seeing because, as far as he could tell,
there was nothing worth seeing.

But suddenly there was.

Directly overhead, in the shadowy crevice between
a strip light and the tile bordering it, something
moved. A spider: black, medium-sized. It launched
itself on a silken thread and began a slow, critical
descent, pausing occasionally to take stock then con-
tinuing on its way. I calculated that if it dropped
another six or seven feet it would land somewhere on
my face and scurry, as arachnids invariably do, into
my open mouth. There it would set up home behind a
crooked palisade of teeth and, on regaining its sang
froid, spin a fine web between my lips in a bid to capture passing prey. An admirable enterprise – bound,
unfortunately, to fail. Rose Cottage was a sterile envi-
ronment, a bug-free zone. The spider was an anomaly. It would starve and eventually die, and my mouth
would be its tomb.

The spider dropped another foot or two, then two more, but not plumb. As Danvers and Jamieson went about their business, the air currents they set up wafted it back and forth. It bobbed at the end of the line like a fisherman's float in choppy waters.

For a while nothing happened, or nothing much. The spider wafted and bobbed, flexing its skinny legs, waiting. I waited, too (really, what choice did I have?).

Then something struck me: a thought so wayward that even Charles l'Orange, in one of his rabid dreams, couldn't have come up with it. What if, instead of sharing my death, the spider, driven by altruism or in error or because of who knows what misguided imperative, imbued my dead flesh with some of its life – a scrap, but just enough. Perhaps, instead of dying, we both might live.

I expected to feel a glimmer of hope, but nothing happened. I didn't even have to wait for it to be dashed.

As the turbulence abated and the spider began its final descent, a hand shot across my field of vision and snatched it from the air. 'Tsk,' said Jamieson in disgust, rubbing the spider between the palms of his hands, destroying it utterly. 'The standard of cleaning in here is a bloody disgrace. Before long we'll be performing autopsies in conditions no better than an abattoir.'

'Wielding cleavers rather than scalpels. Running a cannibal chop shop. Supplying offcuts to dodgy take-aways along the Halifax Road.'

'Don't try to be funny, Danvers, you aren't any good at it. I'm a comic, fabulously endowed, you're nothing but a stooge. You've always been a stooge. The word stooge runs through your long bones like the town's name in a stick of seaside rock.'

In the uneasy silence that followed I could hear the voice recorder whirring. I had the ominous feeling that if it stopped, I would stop, too. Someone had to speak to keep things going and, happily, in the nick of time, someone did.

'Hmm. It rankles, doesn't it, Jamieson, that I beat you to the post of chief pathologist. Hence the insults masquerading as jokes. Still, the best man won; everyone says so, even your wife. Let's wrap this up. Nancy, sweetie, ring the lab and ask your oppo to pencil Starkweather in for the toxicology report. Not Whipple. Beats the hell out of his wife does Whipple. Or she beats him. Perhaps that's how he likes it, some men do. Anyway, he's not always as painstaking as he ought to be, so please let's have Starkweather – though from what I hear, golf club gossip, socially he's a bit of a bore, insists on telling elaborate jokes and loses his way to the punchline.'

'Unlike Whipple.'

'Ho ho. Not bad. Not altogether bad, given that you're not the great comic you think you are.'

'Thank you. I'll savour the praise and discard what's left.'

'So we're done?'

'Doubly done, I'd say.'

'In which case let's be gone –'

'– and let bygones be bygones?'

'That I wouldn't count on, Jamieson, if I were you.'

Nothing more was said.

The whirring ceased.

Jonah

JONAH SAID HE saw his mother grab a needle and skewer a blowfly in zigzag flight. She moved faster than he'd ever seen a human being move before, and while doing so she gave a small sensual grunt. This thrilling display established the scope of his erotic adventures, then and for all time.

To honour her memory he invented the exploding harpoon gun, though inexplicably he failed to patent it.

He spoke of a wife, a singularly accommodating woman that no-one could recall having met, and of twenty (perhaps imaginary) children scattered through time. His youngest boy, Chet, was an unsuccessful door-to-door Bible salesman in Nebraska during the Great Depression. Chet's older siblings, unluckier still, have been lost to posterity. Jonah struggles to remember their names.

Unlike most of his tall stories, which grew ever taller in the telling, the business with the whale was something he spoke of only once, and reluctantly, to his analyst. Having listened carefully to what he had to say, she steepled her fingers and asked him to consider whether the sailors who pitched him into the stormy sea might collectively represent a rejection by his father and, by extension, God; whether the whale in swallowing him had acted, so to speak, maternally, and whether its stomach could, and perhaps should, be deemed a surrogate womb; and whether, when the whale disgorged him onto the shore after a gestation of three days and three nights, it was a kind of rebirth. Jonah, indignant, flew into a rage. He said she'd got it wrong, as badly wrong as all the holy books, WRONG WRONG WRONG in every respect! He shattered a bust of Freud as he stormed out of her office and cancelled all further appointments.

When he arrived in Nineveh, footsore, weary, reeking of sweated brine, his apocalyptic rantings were met not with garlands but derision and a hail of sharp stones – a clear indication of what was to follow.

That night, as he slept in a ditch without the city walls, a dog cocked its leg and sprayed him with urine … and all the while his mind was fizzing with the crazed articles of prophecy and distress.

As for the whale, it dreamt of Jonah only once, after a glut of krill, while suffering from indigestion.

Aquarium Light

1.

THE GOLDFISH SWIMS in his rectangular aquarium. Dreamily, he patrols his world of fake coral, yellow gravel, edible weed, the wreck of a 17th century Spanish galleon, and the shells of several defunct crustaceans. But to Colonel Esquivel's regret, Bolívar, his goldfish, has failed to get to grips with the sulky plough, the vanity mirror, and the numerous educational toys he has so thoughtfully provided.

The colonel raps with a knuckle on the toughened glass, and when Bolívar draws near he says: 'According to intelligence, insurgents are massing darkly like storm clouds in the interior.'

To reward Bolívar for paying attention, he sprinkles a pinch of daphnia on the surface of the water. The aquarium is suffused with light from a Caribbean Blu Glow bulb, by which the colonel, an insomniac, likes to read in the interminable hours after midnight. Bolívar and me, he thinks, keeping each other company while the rest of the world sleeps. Apart from the insurgents, that is. Insurgents never sleep. It's a matter of principle with them.

The colonel sits, reading. He flicks the corner of

each page as he reads, bathed in blue aquarium light. Books on interior design are a firm favourite. Unread intelligence reports are piled high on his desk.

2.

Colonel Esquivel once had long, friendly telephone conversations with the generalissimo, sometimes three a day. He and the generalissimo were on hearty hugs and back-slapping terms. But no more: an unfathomable chill has entered their relationship. The generalissimo seems different from the generalissimo he once knew, or thought he knew. They haven't played golf together for almost six months. Worse still, this year, for the first time in a decade, the generalissimo has failed to send him a birthday card.

Whenever he remembers this, as all too often he does, the colonel experiences a pang. It's a nebulous pang. Because he can't always distinguish between emotions, he doesn't know whether the feeling he's feeling is loss or loneliness (or whether they amount to the same thing), and he doesn't know who could best help him to clarify the situation. Apart from the generalissimo. The generalissimo closely monitors the state's emotional weather and no matter how turbulent it becomes he always responds appropriately. Sometimes he'll gatecrash a village wedding and present a set of steak knives to the furiously blushing bride. At other times people get snatched from the streets, tortured, killed. The generalissimo – so cruel, so capricious. Yet no-one fails to mention his unspeakable charm.

The colonel experiences another pang, and this time it's acute. He has a chestful of medals and a well-drilled regiment, but the solace they provide is meagre. If only he had a wife instead of a goldfish (or as well as a goldfish), a wife ... perhaps then he'd be less inclined to practise a dangerous form of self-abuse involving ceremonial duelling swords. This unsavoury habit has left him scarred for life. After sports he no longer feels comfortable showering with his fellow officers.

3.

The generalissimo has set the colonel an impossible task: single-handedly (i.e., without recourse to his regiment) he must flush the insurgents out of the interior – six hundred square miles of inhospitable and largely uninhabited terrain. But although the colonel searches diligently among rocks and scrub, no insurgents are to be found. Intelligence blames a lack of intelligence, for which no-one is to blame. But as even an illiterate barrio lawyer will tell you: blame must be apportioned, recompense sought.

Esquivel's worst fears are confirmed when he's ordered to return to the capital immediately. The generalissimo is upset. He's declared that not a morsel of food will pass his lips until the colonel has delivered his report. The generalissimo hasn't eaten for three whole days. His food tasters, who are permitted to eat nothing but meals prepared for the generalissimo, are understandably also upset.

The generalissimo stalks the corridors of the presidential palace, his brow a series of compressed ridges, his hands locked so tightly behind his back they're white as bleached bone. An aggressor is massing troops along the western border and spies are monitoring the generalissimo's communications, hoping to detect signs of weakness. The aggressor is known to have the largest army on the continent. If the generalissimo so much as faints from hunger, tanks will cross the border and heads will roll.

4.

In Colonel Esquivel's absence an electrician has entered his townhouse. He hefts the aquarium over by the window then frees a faulty cable from the wall. The cable channels the generalissimo's brand of ultra-nationalism into every home, even homes without electricity.

Apparently, there's some kind of blockage in the wires. It happens all the time. Why else would the population be so restive?

A sniper sends a high-velocity round crashing through the windowpane. Because of flawed intelligence, the insurgents think the colonel is at home, reading books on interior design. Or is this one of the generalissimo's crack marksmen? The electrician has obviously been mistaken for the colonel, perhaps because their moustaches are similar, groomed in a style made popular nearly a century earlier by Emiliano Zapata.

But the bullet fails to hit its intended target. Having barely nicked the lower left-hand corner of the aquarium, it ricochets into an antique mirror, a gift from Isabella of Castile to an Aragonese colonel-ancestor of the colonel's with whom she was purportedly smitten. The mirror shatters cinematically into a thousand priceless fragments. With a startled yelp the electrician quits the room.

After the dust and debris have settled, a chip of glass smaller than a contact lens falls from the lower lip of the aquarium. Water begins to trickle down one leg of the stand and vanish into a crack between the tiles.

5.

The colonel sits despondently among rocks and scrub, of which the country's interior chiefly consists. Ten thousand insurgents could hide here, he thinks, and go openly about their business without fear of detection. In time they could even found an insurgent city, build churches, schools, a hospital, a soccer stadium and an airport, and no-one would notice. The interior is roomy and lacking in, for want of a better word, décor, but it has – he notes, much to his surprise – a thousand potentially attractive features begging to be titivated and enhanced. Rugs, throw cushions, ancillary lighting, sofas, occasional tables and the subtle colour coordination of plants would work wonders on such scrubby terrain. Gigantic mirrors could be installed, to create a feeling of controlled spaciousness. And isn't there, according to the most recent geological survey, an untapped aquifer nearby? The pièce de résistance could be – yes, why not! – an aquarium. The largest in Latin America. An aquarium the size of Lake Poopo.

Six hundred square miles of interior, minus décor. The thought of it makes his moustaches bristle. Perhaps, on reflection, this task outweighs in importance the delivery of his report to the generalissimo. Bad news can always wait. In two or three years he'll return to the capital triumphant, having made the interior, or much of it, habitable. It might then become a top tourist destination, bringing in North American and Canadian dollars. Euros, too. For the first time in the country's history the economy would flourish. In which case the charges laid against him – dereliction of duty, desertion and, most likely, treason – would be quashed, with a raucous laugh, by the generalissimo. He'd kiss him fraternally. They'd resume their Thursday morning rounds of golf and, as always, the colonel would let the generalissimo win – though not by too wide a margin, that would look suspicious.

Meanwhile there's a huge amount of work to be

done. Despite the generalissimo's orders to the contrary, the colonel will summon his regiment – both battalions, reservists included. At present, the men are confined to quarters, lazing around in their underwear, playing desultory hands of poker and paring their fingernails with bayonets. But he's sure they'll rise magnificently to the challenge. A lake-sized aquarium! Just the thought of it will make their moustaches bristle like porcupines.

6.

Although the generalissimo managed to avoid fainting from hunger, he was toppled in a palace coup and replaced by another generalissimo. The new generalissimo is little different from the old one, other than that, every afternoon, he drinks peppermint tea rather than maté – a fact universally known but which the press is not at liberty to report.

When facts are in short supply, rumours abound. One such rumour is that the new generalissimo is actually one of the old generalissimo's lookalikes. But which one? Rumour has it that he had dozens of them. One of the old generalissimo's lookalikes dealt, it was said, with nothing but the country's guava exports; another wore a fancy uniform laden with medals and led the army in ostentatious military displays; yet another wrote books of inscrutable poetry about quarks and quantum mechanics. Other lookalikes were fencing masters, architects, wine connoisseurs, abstract expressionist painters; and each of these specialist lookalikes had an understudy, apprenticed to the art of being a generalissimo lookalike.

Because of this immaculate deception, the generalissimo was perceived to be a man of great stature, one who stood head and shoulders above other world leaders – though in truth he was obliged to wear a corset to correct a deformity of the spine and because he was so short he favoured platform-soled shoes. Even his carpet slippers had lifts.

That the generalissimo was vain was obvious. Every one of his lookalikes had to be younger, taller, suaver, better educated and more eloquent than the generalissimo, who was an ignorant, maladroit lout with, so his critics said from their countries of exile, the table manners of a goat. To avoid the risk of sullying his media image, the generalissimo's advisers suggest that he should never go out in public except in disguise, and preferably not even then.

But surely, runs a popular line of argument, surely the generalissimo died almost a decade ago. As well as being notoriously vain, he was also notoriously lazy. First thing in the morning, last thing at night, one of the lesser lookalikes would squeeze toothpaste onto his toothbrush. Another lesser lookalike would then brush his teeth for him. And when the generalissimo couldn't be bothered to expend even that small amount of energy, as was often the case, the lookalike brushed his own teeth in lieu of the generalissimo's. And wasn't this surrogation taken to extremes? When the generalissimo was fatally ill with heart disease, didn't one of the lookalikes have a triple bypass operation in his stead? Wasn't the generalissimo smuggled out of the palace, post mortem, in the dead of night, and bundled into a river patrolled by one of the most voracious schools of piranha in all of Latin America? – a fate that had befallen many of his enemies and even some of his closest friends.

Ah ... but according to an article in *Tiempos del Mundo*, the new generalissimo has the ability to walk on water, and were a withered limb to be bathed in the golden nectar of his urine it would spontaneously regenerate.

At the Vatican, Cardinal Jose Saraiva Martins, head of the congregation of the causes of saints, is said to be monitoring his progress.

7.

As the blue-lit aquarium water drains away, the oxygenation tube crests the waterline, together with the mastheads and crow's nest of the sunken Spanish galleon. Bolívar's world is shrinking, getting cramped and uncomfortable. Soon the aquarium will no longer sustain piscine life. He'll lie among dry coral and gravel; his flesh will rot away; his bones will splay and bleach in the sun.

The interior of the aquarium is starting to look

uncannily like the interior of the country where Colonel Esquivel, lonely as a rock, awaits the arrival of his regiment. Three of his most trusted aides have been instructed to stop off at his townhouse and pick up Bolívar, the aquarium, and several large sacks of daphnia – *but nothing more*. Not even the colonel's ceremonial duelling swords or a change of underwear. If his men must experience privation, so too will the colonel.

He recalls how, whenever a pinch of daphnia was sprinkled on the surface of the water and Bolívar rose towards it, he felt compelled to withdraw his hand lest he frighten the fish, his friend, his solace. Yet Bolívar rose so eagerly, as if hungering for something more than food. And, in truth, sometimes he merely drew some daphnia between his lips then spat them out, and with a powerful swish of his tail swam away.

Of the numerous attempts made by the insurgents on the lives of the generalissimo, his diplomats, his key advisers, and various high-ranking military personnel, not one has succeeded. Their crowning achievement may be the accidental assassination of a goldfish.

8.

At dawn in the presidential palace the day-shift lookalikes eat breakfast and allocate tasks. Julio, a former night-shift sleeper relegated to the day shift because of insomnia, proffers a bundle of straws of different lengths, the irregular ends sunk in the meat of his fist. The lookalikes each take a straw. When a short straw is drawn, a difficult or potentially dangerous task has to be undertaken. A long straw – such as the one Nestor has drawn – denotes a mundane task. In this case, between 11.10-11.20am, Nestor has to be photographed wearing the upper half of a full dress uniform, so that later in the week the generalissimo can renew his passport.

Excluded from the draw is one of the specialist lookalikes known as a soundalike: Luis, who studied at the Sorbonne and speaks a French so exquisite it would make Marcel Proust shiver like an aspen. What's more, he sounds just like the generalissimo speaking French – something the generalissimo himself patently cannot do. At 5.00pm, Luis will meet with the French ambassador, his lady wife, and a delegation of French mineralogists. Each of the mineralogists has an expensive gift for the generalissimo. They and the ambassador are hoping to persuade him to let them plunder the extensive mineral deposits in the interior.

And what of Ramos, who drew the shortest straw? His task is to cut the ceremonial ribbon and deliver a speech at a small nuclear power facility. It's the smallest facility of its kind in the world, operated by children. 'They'll treat it as a toy, and it will teach them about responsibility,' he says, reading aloud from the text that one of the generalissimo's crack speech writers has prepared on his behalf. His fellow lookalikes offer a mocking round of applause. Then 'Vamos, Ramos!' they cry, for one of the armour-plated presidential limousines has driven up, accompanied by a pistolero gang of leather-clad motorcycle outriders. The facility has been sited a long way from the capital, near the western border, where easterlies constantly blow. If – God forbid! – there should be an uncontrolled discharge of radioactive material, a gentle breeze will deliver it safely into the country next door.

But radiation sickness is among the least of Ramos's worries, though with the dregs of his coffee he gulps down a precautionary iodine pill. Attempts on the generalissimo's life are an almost daily occurrence, and the insurgents have become increasingly bold. Consider the fate of poor Eduardo. He'd no sooner stepped onto the balcony overlooking the presidential square than a grenade – fired by a slingshot, according to the generalissimo's top ballistics expert – struck him full in the chest. Having kept goal for one of the country's most admired soccer teams, Eduardo acted instinctively: he caught the grenade on the rebound, whereupon it exploded, blowing him to pieces. Smithereened body parts and a shower of blood rained down on the square. The crowd let out a fearful moan. The real generalissimo, hidden behind bulletproof drapes, caught the shattered torso of his lookalike as it was hurled by the force of the explosion through the open French windows and into the state room. Down below, in the square, there was pandemonium. Tanks were swiftly manoeuvred into position, blocking all access roads. Realising that something was expected of them, soldiers began to fire indiscriminately into the crowd. Amid screams, gunshots and mounting panic, the generalissimo strode onto the balcony, covered in blood but miraculously whole. Slowly, with supreme authority, he raised his arms to quell the crowd's cries of anguish and exultation.

The lookalikes on the day shift have become accustomed to terror, but is it any wonder they harbour resentments? Their night-shift colleagues are pampered, lazy. Each and every one of them retires to a different bed each night, and his sole task is to sleep soundly for at least eight hours, otherwise the generalissimo won't feel sufficiently rested.

9.

The regiment is in its underwear, confined to quarters. Every fingernail has been pared, every last toenail cut. A mountain of surplus nail has been deposited in a bin by the latrine. Even Hector, parrot and regimental mascot, has had his claws clipped – perhaps too close for comfort. Unable to perch, he's hunkering sullenly on the floor of his cage. Time lacks meaning in the barrack room. Fifty thousand desultory hands of cards have been played, in the course of which the playing cards have become almost featureless, reduced to tatters.

If only the colonel would march onto the base and

issue a few orders – Colonel Esquivel, with those distinguished flecks of grey in his hair and his bygone era matinee-idol looks. To the men who serve under him he is many things: a surrogate father, a war hero, a bona fide revolutionary icon. And sometimes something more ...

After lights out, while their compadres sleep, it's not unknown for new conscripts to remove from the shelf in their bedside locker, beneath handkerchiefs and the statutory clean pair of white cotton shorts, a framed photograph of the colonel, and kiss it fervently again and again. Self-manipulation or even self-mutilation of the genitals may ensue. Likewise muffled sobs. Those in adjacent beds quickly learn to ignore such things.

But in an unscheduled bulletin, the generalissimo has just announced, with deep regret, the following news: Colonel Octavio Esquivel has been killed in a most barbaric fashion – stoned by insurgents. As yet, it has not been possible to recover his body, though a team of French mineralogists at work in the interior has volunteered to bring him home. Once that is done, the colonel will be buried with full military honours, and as a mark of respect his many books on interior design will be housed in a new extension to the state library, to be called the Esquivel Culture Wing.

The regiment would like to mourn, but no order has been given to that effect.

10.

Daphnia on the surface of the water, dappling the light. When Bolívar rises, the hand that sprinkles the daphnia withdraws. Is there, thinks Bolívar, an aquarium in the afterlife, an aquarium of infinite capacity? Does it contain coral, weed and gravel, a Spanish galleon and myriad trappings indicative of prosperity and success? How blue will the water be? Is there really such a thing as a hand that forever sprinkles daphnia and never, ever withdraws?

Democracy

THERE HE IS, mopping his face theatrically, using a handkerchief as big as a tablecloth, the gleam of sidereal light on his brow. No, he's way over there by a stand of trees, the scallywag, addressing a goat – a nanny, I believe – in a most cordial manner. During a twenty-eight-day period almost one thousand sightings were logged. Their veracity has been established with the use of a polygraph.

Occasionally, while rummaging through trash cans in the early hours, he gets mistaken for a bear – a large, hirsute man in a tatty racoonskin coat. As the tranquilliser dart pricks his thigh, he laughs, we all laugh, though his is a hearty boom and ours a nervous titter.

Yet, tranquillised, he sprints from the scene. He runs like electricity, so light of foot that native trackers cannot follow him.

Our laughter sounds hollow then, our demeanour becomes stern.

The adults who refused to submit to the polygraph were beaten with iron bars. While we brutalised and dismembered the toys, in accordance with the Torquemada manual, we made the children watch.

Truth will out.

But then we see him on TV, before the world's press, threatening to declare war on Switzerland ... and Swaziland, too, if such a place exists. He laughs. Everyone laughs, they're not sure why. The translators laugh, too, having nothing to translate but laughter. The flashguns of a ravenous pack of paparazzi are triggered as one, obscuring his means of escape. Temporarily blinded, we ask ourselves: *Is this really how a Minister for Foreign Affairs should behave?*

On misty mornings he uses the lake as a mirror. We find his scat among the trees, still warm to the touch. Of him: no trace.

Those who failed the polygraph test had their houses demolished. Their furniture was dragged into the streets and smashed to matchwood. Nothing is allowed to hinder our quest for truth, we are renowned for it the world over.

Later he was seen consorting with rogues, villains, scoundrels, thugs, scapegraces and desperados, a veritable mafia of them. On one occasion he appeared, the scamp, to be trying to sell his father's medals. (His father the war hero.) By his side stood the regimental goat, nuzzling his hand.

What are we to make of this? Ours is a fledgling democracy, and the nation looks to him for guidance.

The children of those who failed the polygraph test were fostered out to cannibals. Although he has spoken against this practice, spoken eloquently and with great conviction, still we persist. Old habits die hard.

But no man who venerates truth can claim to be without flaws. While he was operating a faulty mind-set, lightning razed his neighbour's barn.

Unnatural Order

THERE WAS A device for unhooking the lower jaw and replacing it with a refrigerator door.

Tongue like flypaper, breath like rotting meat.

One eye had eagle acuity, the other (industrial accident) drew an annuity.

A thin metal cone instead of a nose, beak-like, to spear larks in flight.

Who could have foreseen, in Alfred Nobel's day, the role of dynamite in dentistry.

Each mercury-filled tooth was a radio receiver and lightning crackled in the maw.

The Siblings Jones

DEEP IN DAVY JONES's locker there's a scroll commemorating his late brother Casey, train wreck hero of popular renown. Davy, malevolent spirit of the seven seas, has borne many a shipwrecked sailor to a watery grave. But his behaviour is as nothing compared to Casey's satyrical philanderings, his monstrous drunken guilt, the way he whittled on the glans of his penis with a craft knife until, erect, it looked like an intricately carved mahogany baluster, and in repose like a decaying vegetable. Had Casey been fired from his job on the Illinois Central Railroad, he could easily have joined the next freak show that passed through Water Valley. Of which Davy knew nothing. To this day he mourns the loss of his only brother.

But living in the ocean depths poses its own problems. Davy feels the cold more acutely than when he was young, and over the years he's been obliged to shift his house nearer and nearer to a geothermal vent. The sulphurous stench used to bother him, but now he barely notices it. Hot water streams constantly through the windows and doors and exits via cracks in the walls. His house badly needs caulking.

Frankly, it also needs a woman's touch. That's another thing Davy wouldn't know about.

Unless Casey's widow, Janie, gets her way, that is. She'd always been fond of Davy. The way she picked strands of dried sargassum out of his hair was noted by everyone, Casey included, which triggered another unhappy bout of philandering and whittling. She even claims to enjoy the company of Davy's boon companions: the swordfish, the giant squid, the great white shark, all of whom relish the human titbits he provides them with. Janie they give cold appraisal. Is she food or not? Only time will tell.

No-one knows why Casey didn't leap to safety, why he held on to the brake lever after it was locked in position, after the engine was put in reverse, after the sanders were opened, and as the train slithered down the track towards disaster. The official report into the train wreck declined to speculate as to why engineer Jones remained on the footplate. According to Davy, Casey was wrestling with the brake lever as with a laocoonian sea serpent. Or suchlike. Davy lives in a state of almost constant hallucination. But when reality is so strange, who can tell the difference?

The equinoctial tides are running high, higher than ever before. Towering waves crash together. Spray mists the face of the moon. Even in the ocean depths this turbulence is felt. The water slews one way then another, and during a particularly powerful surge Janie is swept off her feet and dumped, fishnet stockings and all, into Davy's lap. The nautical chart he was consulting sashays to the floor.

Janie and Davy happily ensconced. Another storey has been added to the house. In the inky night (marginally inkier than the inky day), Davy works downstairs while Janie sleeps restlessly overhead, dreaming turbid dreams, her legs entwined in sheets of woven kelp. He's keen, as ever, to finish the task and join her in their bed of sponge and seaweed, but his concentration is shot. He's finding it hard to tally up, harder still to reconcile his joy with the sailors' last words, their pitiful cries and exclamations.

An architectural peculiarity of the house is a narrow staircase, an inch or two wide, up which Davy's pet eel, Casanova, slithers.

Trelawney the Lion-Tamer

DESPITE HIS PRECARIOUS foothold on the garden roller, Trelawney can see, between one snagged corner of the venetian blind and the windowsill, through an aperture with all the clammy allure and disappointment of a pier-end peep show, someone making love to his mother. A cold night. His breath mists the windowpane. Steam engine noises are coming from within – they've left the television on, loud. A documentary about rail travel in China, interrupted by adverts. The man has hairy buttocks, as most men do; they rise and fall with alarming regularity. No visible tattoos. Not a seaman, then. Sailors adorn chest and upper arms rather than buttocks, thinks Trelawney; mermaids and anchors, a large four-master, full sail, nipples doubling as cannon. The fetishistic iconography of the senior service.

Years pass. Trelawney now has tats of his own – small, discreetly situated cartoon characters: Foghorn Leghorn, Yosemite Sam, Deputy Dawg, each of them framed in their sprocketed rectangles of celluloid like old masters. On his right shoulder he bears a tat of his estranged wife; a good likeness. Occasionally he turns round to kiss it. His nipples are pierced twice through and festooned, at weekends, with little gold bells on short lengths of chain. His scrotal sac is pierced and hung with miniature ornamental teacups, connected at the handles by a sagging loop of chain that, on close inspection, is fashioned out of tiny teaspoons. His foreskin is pierced in nine places and fitted with rings and bells. Erections tend to jangle, muffled, in his underwear. He's plagued by a nipple infection and a nasty rash but can't quite bring himself to visit the company's physician, Dr Phlox.

Night after night he dreams of bells. Not the sight of them, swinging powerfully, elegantly, as they do in the cathedral at Notre Dame; sound only. And bowl gongs, weirdly tinny, as though issuing from a cheap transistor radio. He makes the mistake of mentioning this to his mother. His mother hints that his father is a Buddhist – a supreme patriarch, no less – then maddeningly declines to elaborate. A man would never do that. Nor would most women. Only mothers; those for whom post-partum psychosis is a lifelong affliction. His mother also hints that his father is the actor Charles Laughton. Trelawney rejects this, sensibly, on the grounds that Laughton is dead, died, in fact, years before he was born. He checks his birth certificate to make sure and scours a biography of the actor. Finally he hunts under L in his mother's address book. Nothing. No Lawtons, Lowtons, Lutons, or even Leytons, though mysteriously one of the L-pages has been torn out. The indentations on the following page are indecipherable. He doesn't know whether to be disappointed or relieved: the bastard son of a famous man, the reflected glory, the responsibilities it would entail. His bell dreams continue, accompanied by white flickering visuals, like an old cathode-ray TV set after the programmes had ended.

Trelawney comes awake on the sofa. Abe is standing naked in the doorway, striking elegant pose #29 in the 1962 deportment manual for *Playboy* bunnies, Las Vegas edition, described therein as 'demure but with undoubted allure'. Trelawney calls out: 'Why, hello there, Judy Garland!' To which Abe counters: 'Well met, Peggy Lee!' Their role models in life, the life they lead at weekends and during holidays. They've shared this camp sense of humour since childhood but kept it strictly to themselves. As he moves, Abe's body jewellery clanks, rattles and chimes. He's just finished shaving his chest, which is slightly inflamed under a sunbed tan. He has many more tats than Trelawney, but mostly in obscure places: in his armpits, under his tongue, on the soles of his feet. Neither Trelawney nor Abe is remotely homosexual. Nor, for that matter, bisexual. Sex doesn't come into it. Abe is married to Lindy, a corporate lawyer based in Singapore for much of the year. Lindy is away at present, merging conglomerates. The rain falls steadily; the central heating is on high. Champagne chills in a silver ice-bucket. Servants so discreet they're all but invisible are setting the table for dinner. Trelawney is naked, too. Abe is Trelawney's house guest while his apartment is being refurbished.

They discuss their relative problems. Abe declares he has none, though he has – who hasn't? But he doesn't want to burden Trelawney. He's rich, happily married, in the best of health, mentally and physically. A little particle of God is nestled within him: a 5-watt glow of spiritual contentment. He's handsome, too, with a beautifully styled shock of blue-black hair. 'Perhaps,' he says, coming up with something suitably trivial, 'the interior designer that Lindy and I hired, a celebrated cocaine fiend with a Louis XIV sense of scale, will demolish a party wall and my notoriously litigious neighbour, Lord Rhubarb-Rhubarb of Ripon, will sue.'

This, they both think, is conjectural. It therefore doesn't count.

Trelawney, however, is bereft of body hair due to alopecia universalis and his wife will neither live with him nor seek a divorce. She's a lapsed Catholic who has unlapsed and relapsed many times, a hedonist in love with incense, ritual and guilt. She despises all men bar the clergy. Some clergy. And Graham Greene. Despite having died in 1991, Greene is still frequently spotted in various parts of the world, often at two locations simultaneously. He's said to consult her on his trips to London, returning, fortified and enlightened, to his villa in Antibes. He finds her furious on/off Catholicism bracing. She demands money from Trelawney, increasingly large sums of money, and hints that Greene is thinking of putting him in a novel. He'll be a dissolute character, a moral bankrupt, seedy as sin, his identity thinly disguised. Even people who don't know Trelawney will know it's him. His mother has agreed to supply his wife, and hence Greene, with screeds of damning information about her son. What's more, his mother is on the brink of converting to Catholicism. She's taking advice and instruction from, among others, Mr Greene. Finally, his wife and his mother have moved in together. They are, so he gathers, bosom pals, and perhaps something more.

All of which, naturally, comes as a blow. Trelawney performs an important and highly sensitive role within the Financial Conduct Authority (FCA). He's the press liaison officer for a team of regulators. They investigate allegations of financial misconduct before deciding that, on the balance of evidence, there's no case to answer. He gives successful press briefings. He must defend the FCA's decision – always the same decision – resolutely, implacably, before hostile left-wing journalists baying for blood.

As a child actor at the Sicilia Conte school, he was a frustrated spear carrier, destined never to secure a leading role. Abe played Peter Pan, Hamlet, one of the brothers Karamazov, Don Quixote and St George. Trelawney, who failed the audition for the role of Sancho Panza and instead became half of Rocinante, was only slightly jealous, and temporarily at that. After all, Abe was his best friend and a fellow nipple-piercer. But despite his actorly incompetence, Trelawney's future employers recognised in him a unique set of qualities. Not talents, he had none. Qualities. His calm and calming demeanour. His effortless blandishments. He was thirteen years old when they singled him out. They paid his school fees and a substantial annual retainer. They were avuncular, jolly and ruthless. They co-opted his mother and arranged for her to be locked up, albeit briefly, in the cushiest of asylums, akin to a luxury health spa, and submitted an application to become his legal guardians. Money surreptitiously changed hands and the application was approved. Though the outlay was considerable, it was, after all, an investment. When Trelawney lost his hair almost overnight (fistfuls on his pillow, blocking the shower drain, whisked along the platform as a tube train entered the station) they remained unperturbed. Elderly, grey, they've been imperturbable for more than half a century. Their plans extend well into the next millennium and beyond. They offer advice on fiscal policy to Presidents Obama and Putin, and give sure-fire racing tips to Elizabeth II, not that she needs them. Their knowledge and expertise is ever in demand and never found wanting. They suggest to Trelawney that he should wear a tawny hairpiece for public appearances. This he does. He's known to free market economists the world over as Trelawney the lion-tamer. But after hours, in the executive washroom, bald as a coot, he's often mistaken for the janitor.

Abe emails Lindy and she fires back: *Trelawney's wife's demands are blackmail pure and simple!*

What should Trelawney do?

The rash has now spread from groin to thigh.

⊖

Every Sunday evening, in preparation for the working week, Trelawney unclips and unbuckles himself from his collection of chains, bells, bangles, rings, belts and studs, most of which are crafted in gold and encrusted with precious stones. Some of the bangles are antique, Ghanaian, Ethiopian, heirlooms from destitute royal households, carved from the bones of extinct species, wound with human hair and fine gold thread. Though each is insured for a five-figure sum, they're of much greater personal value. Not senti- mental; sentimentality doesn't come into it. Trelawney never had a pet, a brother or a sister. He doesn't believe in God. He tries not to think about his mother; her icy heart. She expelled him from her womb like a turd, she said, and flatly denied him the milk from her breasts. Knowledge of this makes him unhappy, but more than that: numb. He collects jew- ellery, mutilates his body and adorns himself at weekends. He finds solace in adopting the persona of Peggy Lee and hums *Fever* in the shower.

This makes him feel, at least temporarily, whole, complete.

As he removes these precious artefacts from his body, and lays them reverentially on one of the living- room windowsills, he sobs. He tries to. His body convulses but the tears won't come. The ultra-discreet servants have been given West End theatre tickets, to get them off the premises. Diplomatically, Abe has retired to his bedroom and is listening to the radio. Every light in the house has been turned down or off. In the bedroom, on the radio, Big Ben strikes twelve. Outside, in Westminster, the chimes echo over the rooftops. Trelawney's heart is heavy. He lowers the blind without noticing that the sash window is slightly open, leaving a thin aperture through which cool air enters the room.

As, next day, while Trelawney and Abe are at work, does a burglar.

Trelawney finds all his jewellery missing. Not a single gold safety pin remains. Beside a photo of his estranged and vengeful wife, hell bent on extortion, there's a brief note: 'say what, mista, yor wifes a stuna and got prety good taste.' The portrait is smeared with a snail track of dried semen. A police constable picks up the note with a pair of tweezers and drops it into an evidence bag. The photo in its frame goes into another. Unthinkingly, he whistles several choruses of *One for My Baby* while walking round the flat, admiring the expensive fixtures and fittings. Meanwhile his colleague explains about forensics and their department's new graphology consultant, Grace Zappettini. A character profile will be built up, he says, computer records scanned. The detectives are young, brash, confident. They say they expect to apprehend the culprit within the next twenty-four hours. Trelawney is duly impressed.

The details are emailed to Lindy, who replies: *Your wife will have had something to do with this. Try to get to the bottom of it. The police are useless. Hire a private detective!*

Incisive and perspicacious, as always. Trelawney sometimes wishes Lindy had married him instead of Abe. That, alas, could never be. Lindy likes tall men, well-muscled, broad across the shoulders, with a good head of hair. Trelawney is a hairless pocket-Adonis, not her type at all. Lindy and Abe; so far apart yet so much together.

But Lindy and Abe have troubles, too, of course. Due to the rigours and complexities of their working lives, they spend less than two hours together every month. 'Hardly long enough for a slap-up meal and a good shag,' laughs Abe; but behind his laughter lies sorrow. Lindy has a strong genetic predisposition towards ovarian cancer. Her mother died from it at the age of forty-two. Lindy is thirty-nine and the alarm on her biological clock is set. They are gnawingly lonely, often on separate continents, in vastly different time zones.

Trelawney's left nipple is infected, swollen, clogged with a milky pus that seeps into his shirt. The problem is becoming acute. He's had to remove the tiny gold sleepers that keep the piercings open. A sticking plaster has been applied, holding in place a blob of antiseptic cream, but to no discernible improvement. He wonders how much longer he can avoid visiting Dr Phlox, a lush with bar room halitosis and a mischievously wagging tongue. Whatever the good doctor knows, everyone knows, and his exaggerations are hugely inventive and cruelly barbed. Something his employers approve of. It boosts tension, which, given a little prod here, a push there, becomes creative tension. Staff suicides have increased in number since the good doctor took up his post, but the standard of work has improved no end. Employees aren't allowed to visit any doctor other than Phlox; it's written into their contract. They live in perpetual fear of becoming unwell.

Several times a day, Trelawney locks the door of the executive washroom and dries his shirt under the hot-air dryer. It leaves a stain, a faint concentric circle like a target over his heart.

⊖

'You are, and have always been, the arse-end in the pantomime horse of our marriage!' To amplify that statement, she slammed the door behind her. Trelawney's wife, obviously. That was two years ago, the last time he saw her. Since then, nothing but long distance vitriol: nasty anonymous notes postmarked Wimbledon, the lettering cut from lurid Sunday newspaper headlines or stencilled and coloured in with a child's unruly hand. Since then, every month without fail, his lawyer has transferred monies to her lawyer on his behalf. Both lawyers bill him for this service. Direct contact has become impossible. His wife acknowledges these payments with abuse.

Her charge was no mere conceit. At the age of fifteen, an anxious stripling virgin, Trelawney inhabited Rocinante's hindquarters in the Sicilia Conte end-of-year production of *Don Quixote*. She had been given the more demanding role at the front end. For six rehearsals prior to the performance they stripped down to their underwear and entered the heavy, sweaty hide; and while she stood much as normal inside the suit (though slightly bent at the waist), he was obliged to lean forward until his brow nestled in the small of her back. He planted his hands, of necessity, on her hips. Yes, necessity; you need lockstep coordination to make a plausible Rocinante out of two adolescents in a baggy horse suit. Her hips were an all-important factor in synchronising their movements. A slight twitch of the muscles in her left buttock, or a tensing of the right hip, and he knew precisely when to lift his legs to match or countermand hers. Sometimes, when setting off, they imitated a spider walk, or gave a synchronised shuffle. Sometimes they swapped legs mid-stride for variety and comic effect.

The dance routines were the most demanding part of the show. At one point he had to run round her several times, making drunken staggers, while pirouetting her, daintily, on the spot. Then there was the Fred Astaire number; and the rhumba, for which they were joined by the rest of the cast. In the suit, under the hot lights, they sweated like crazy; it ran in rivulets down her backbone and joined the copious exudations from his scalp and brow; it trickled down the bridge of his nose and dripped past the waistband of her knickers into the dark, mysterious cleft between her buttocks. His palms were perpetually moist with excitement and tension. Her hips were warm and slithery.

London was in the grip of a heatwave that summer. In public parks sparrows in their thousands fell from the trees. People collapsed in the streets, on buses, at work. Under the stage lights, in the horse suit, the heat was unbearable. By the third rehearsal, unbeknown to the director, his assistants, and other members of the cast, they dispensed with clothes entirely. In the dressing room she gave his nipple rings a long, cool look but said nothing. What, after all, was there to say? He hadn't the courage to return her stare. But from time to time, trapped in Rocinante's skin, he'd become aware of the pendulous swaying ascent of his penis, swishing back and forth through the charged and humid air. There was a musty smell, too, that was faintly disgusting but oddly stirring.

Despite the discomfort it entailed, he looked forward with mounting pleasure to each of the rehearsals, particularly the moment when, flushed with exertion, they left the stage and trotted along to the changing room. The rest of the cast would be onstage for ten minutes more, until the curtain came down. This, then, was a moment all their own, a moment in which to praise each other, compare notes, apologise for a slight misstep or a late cue. Mostly, however, they stood at the centre of the room, breathing heavily, saying nothing, caught up in their own puzzled thoughts, till one of them reached for the zipper and the claustrophobic suit fell away, leaving them chilled, naked, and ever so slightly embarrassed. Back to back, they towelled themselves off and clambered into their clothes, including the t-shirts marked ROCINANTE FORE and ROCINANTE AFT, in readiness for the curtain call.

The performance they gave on the final night, before an audience swollen with theatrical agents, their catamites and minions, was the best by far; a performance with lashings of wit and panache that had, act by act, been hooted to the rafters. Trelawney was exhilarated as they passed swiftly along the short corridor to their changing room; he felt tingly and light-headed. His partner's hips undulated moistly beneath his fingers; every inch of her body seemed to offer a lubricious thrill. Soft panting noises were coming, slightly muffled, from the front of the suit. His thighs and stomach were remarkably cool, even slightly clammy. His phallus swayed leadenly, danger-ously, drawing massive reserves of blood from the surrounding tissue. The Nureyev and Fonteyn of the pantomime horse; their skilful co-ordination was rapidly breaking down. He could hardly make one foot follow on from the other.

As they turned into the changing room their ankles locked and he sprawled heavily on top of her, his chin coming to rest just behind her left ear, his face in her hair. But the most surprising thing occurred just below the waistline. His erection buckled on impact with her body, encountered a momentary resistance, then slid gracefully, slickly to rest. Immediately there was a surge in his loins and a rush of heat passed through him. His partner lay still, giving occasional gentle shivers, breathing lightly. It was over in an instant. He levered himself off her body, unzipped the suit and released his head and shoulders. She sat up, turned to face him, and said: 'Now look what you've done. You're going to have to marry me.' Her eyes were sinister blue chips inside the horse's head.

Shocked by what had happened, he replied, without a moment's thought, 'Okay, I will.'

And when both had turned sixteen, with the approval of their guardians, they did.

⊖

Trelawney returns from the office somewhat earlier than usual, pours himself a large scotch and soda, slumps into an armchair and begins to contemplate the mess his life is in. His so-called life. He broods to no good purpose, sipping whisky. He shuffles and squirms, enveloped in plush leather. The area around his groin itches horribly. There's also a large, uncomfortable bulge in his hip pocket, a plain buff envelope stuffed with bills of high denomination – the 'gratuity' that, as if by magic, appears in the bottom drawer of his desk every month. Trelawney has had a new hi-security lock fitted to the drawer; the key remains on his person at all times. Nevertheless, the gratuities continue to appear, without fail, on the 29th of the month. This adds to his general feeling of unease.

A car backfires in the street. Big Ben strikes the hour. Right on cue, clouds mass over Westminster and rain begins to fall. The room has darkened considerably, a rheostat dip; everything becomes either more or less than it was just a moment ago – more two-dimensional, less substantial, altogether less real. The glass in his hand with its half-inch of oily amber liquid has an illusory quality, like a stage prop. A suitable ambience for a haunting, thinks Trelawney. This is when his unknown father should appear, shaking his gory locks – presuming he's dead, of course, and slain. 'Let's face it,' mutters Trelawney, 'gory locks are for thesps, that preening gang of ne'er-do-wells!' But he's not really sure this is what he believes. It makes him sound too much like his mother. A depressing thought.

Meanwhile, his scrotum is on fire. He applies calamine lotion to the infected area with a cotton wool ball. The lotion is an exaggerated shade of pink, like an embalmers' cosmetic; it trickles coolly, dries and cracks. As he walks, it flakes into his underwear. He feels desperately weary, stressed and upset. What wouldn't I give to get away for a while, thinks Trelawney. But he remembers the last holiday he took with his wife. They visited the Mato Grosso. On the first evening, as the sun went down, the animals began to screech and scream. It was hideous, relentless. Worse still were the insect noises: mandible chatter; chitinous bodies resonant as drums; clickings, whirrings, scratchings, multiplied a thousand-fold. The individual sounds merged into a roar, like a waterfall crashing onto rocks. By the time darkness fell they could barely hear each other and sleep was impossible. The cabin vibrated to a low, destructive frequency; about 50-Hz, Trelawney reckoned. A guess, nothing more, but his wife didn't much care for it. The timber walls shivered; insect corpses rained down on the mosquito net. Dust shivered into a hanging cloud several inches above the floor. Crockery rattled on the shelves, the cutlery in the drawers. Lightbulbs jiggled at the end of their cords. Outdoors the sound was even worse; not perhaps quite so reminiscent of a waterfall, more like an earthquake. After three exhausting days they caught a plane home and slept for twenty-four hours. When they woke they argued. The door slammed. She had gone.

When he checks his email, the first message is from his wife. It reads: *Your mother is dangerously ill and asking for you. Come at once!*

But where? His wife's new address is a closely guarded secret. He contacts his lawyer, who telephones her lawyer, who refuses to divulge that information. It is, he says, confidential; revealing her whereabouts would be a violation of the trust between him and his client, whose wishes are of paramount importance. The police are just as unhelpful; this isn't, he's told, a criminal matter. He scours the phone book and the electoral register. He calls a friend who works for the Met's traffic division and has him run a discreet trace on her car. 'Sold eighteen months ago to a man in Cardiff,' he's told. The man in question, tracked down to his place of work, is as helpful as can be, but, he says, the registration documents were destroyed in a house fire (the work of an arsonist, apparently), and all he can recall of her address is the location: 'South London ... Putney, Wandsworth, somewhere in that region. A biggish house on a corner. Near an undertaker's and a row of shops.' Trelawney is, above all and despite everything, a dutiful, loving son, and becoming more frantic by the minute. He contacts another friend, an underwriter, who phones a friend of a friend in financial services who investigates her credit rating using her last known address. No debts outstanding; no current address on file. He calls every last one of her friends, her family and acquaintances, and encounters nothing but dead lines, rudeness, wrong numbers and voicemail. He tries to get an SOS message read out on Radio 4, but fails; they don't do that any more. On the advice of the manager of his local CAB (Citizens Advice Bureau), he phones her favourite bookshops and restaurants, her chiropodist, her acupuncturist, her florist, her French polisher, her hairstylist, her haberdasher, her manicurist, her dietician, even her internet service provider. He phones animal charities to which he knows she makes, or made, donations. He phones every department store and beauty salon in the West End of London. He phones Battersea Dogs' Home. He phones a branch of the Samaritans at which, inconceivably, she did some voluntary work, about two week's worth, in 2003 or '04. He's flustered, close to tears, and they misinterpret the nature of his call. As he tries to explain for the third or fourth time another email arrives. It reads: *Ha! Ha!*

These are the torments Trelawney endures.

His wife says Mr Greene is visiting London incognito. He's filled notebook after notebook with details of Trelawney's scurrility, and even he, a man who has chronicled some of the darkest aspects of human nature in the most inhospitable places on Earth, is said to raise an occasional eyebrow at the things Trelawney's mother relates. It's said that Trelawney has a secret life; that during fake petit mal seizures he commits unspeakable acts.

In his dreams, Trelawney scrubs his hands again and again until they are transparent; he leans against a table, reading a newspaper, and the newsprint can clearly be seen through them – terrible headlines full of cruelty, devastation and death. Guilt leadens his bones. His work has begun to suffer, but as yet none of his colleagues has noticed, or, if noticed, said anything about it. The rash now stretches, pinkly, itchily, in a welt from his neck to the back of his knees. All rings and studs have been removed from his body. Inside his clothes he feels chafed.

Weekends are by far the worst. He hasn't the requisite joie de vivre to sing along with his Peggy Lee CDs. In truth, her three-minute epics of unrequited love, her resilience in the face of adversity, her thrillingly facile joys and woes, no longer speak to him. Perhaps he's getting old. He finds himself listening to radio phone-ins, especially programmes dealing with medical matters, but no-one seems to share his problem. Even Abe, his friend and confidant, has more or less deserted him; he now spends most of his time with the interior designer who has, apparently, a suitcaseful of interesting outtakes from *The Wizard of Oz*, including a backstage sequence showing Judy/ Dorothy's breasts being bound to make her look less like a woman, more like a child. The designer, a bondage fetishist with a particular interest in bandages, who sponsors clandestine archaeological digs in the Valley of the Kings, has refurbished Abe's apartment as a 19th century Crimean hospital ward. Battered metal cots occupy every room (nine in the master bedroom alone!), draped with rough grey blankets complete with realistic bloodstains. The walls have been thinly lime-washed to allow plaster to show through; damp patches and mould have been carefully painted in. Clockwork rats patrol the skirting boards; wax dummies inhabit the beds. Wooden crutches, trepanning equipment, surgical tools, bed-pans and hand-finished rubber-moulded leeches in chipped enamel pots add an air of authenticity. And bandages – bandages galore, needless to say. The lounge, however, is the pièce de résistance: a shrine to Florence Nightingale that includes several authenticated letters, her well-thumbed Bible, one of her bonnets, an ivory comb, her favourite brass syringe, and a lock of her hair. Numerous photographs of Florence have been mounted in gunmetal frames and arranged in date order on the chimney breast wall. Soldiers' and nurses' uniforms in the Victoria and Albert Museum are being replicated swiftly and at great cost. Abe hopes to have everything ready for Lindy's next trip to London. As yet she knows nothing of these plans. She thinks the walls are being rag rolled. She thinks a super-efficient Swedish log-burning stove is being installed. It will be something of a surprise.

On a blustery July day – the 12th, his birthday – Trelawney finds himself swaying drunkenly on a latticed metal service gantry high above the city. He can't remember how he got up there, or why. It seems he's lost one of his shoes; also its accompanying sock. Perhaps he threw them into the Thames. His shirt tail snaps like a flag in the wind. Some four or five feet away, on the roof of the building, a fireman is uttering soothing, nonsensical words, the kind of thing one would say to calm a skittery horse. Far below, in the plaza, an eager crowd has gathered to witness his destruction. Some of the spectators are much too close, almost directly beneath him; the police keep shepherding them back behind a gaily fluttering line of tape, but others keep surging forward. Nearby, the river makes a casual loop round the Isle of Dogs; an ebb tide, boats struggling upstream. In the distance, Trelawney can see the Kent marshes, flat countryside, patchwork fields. His tie keep slapping against the side of his head, making his eyes smart.

There's a commotion further back on the roof and someone is ushered forward. Suddenly his wife is there, beside the fireman. She's wearing a blue woollen two-piece, Jackie Onassis style, with cream piping round the lapels, and holding her lustrous hair in a thick hank to stop it from blowing in the wind. 'Come home,' she says to Trelawney, 'all will be well.' She gives him a tight little smile and reaches out with her free hand. On the third finger her wedding band glints: a diamond cluster honing the light to its own perfect symmetry.

That's all it takes.

There's no hesitation.

He climbs up, stretching his hand towards hers, spanning the void between them.

$$\ominus$$

The police, having interviewed Trelawney in the presence of his lawyer and Dr Phlox, decide to let the matter rest. But his employers will not hear of an immediate return to work; he must, absolutely *must*, for his own good, for the sake of his health and his reputation, take an extended period of leave. Rest and respite, that's what's needed. They are now noticeably less avuncular and more distant; evidently his star has waned. Their secretaries send him flowers and pp'd get well soon cards, though his requests to return to work are firmly but politely rejected. Every day they send flowers by the vanload. Wilting blooms are everywhere, stacked on tables, piled up in the hallway; they fill every vase in the house, the sinks, the basins, the baths, the shower, the bidet. Their smell is funereal. Shed petals litter the floor. Trelawney worries about his future prospects, whether his next gratuity will linger in the bottom drawer for his successor to find.

Things don't go well at home. Abe, who can't abide Trelawney's wife, remains in his apartment, unfinished though it is. He gives Trelawney a parting gift: a stand of replica rifles, circa 1872. Lindy sends an email which reads: *Hang in there, buster!* Kind. Understated. Typical Lindy. His wife, who never tried to get along with her, deletes the message before he's had a chance to read it. She scratches his Peggy Lee CDs. She dismisses the servants without consulting him and sneers at his chemically suppressed rage. Cappuccino froth – that's what she calls it. Every afternoon a nurse arrives to check his medication and treat his infection and rash. The latter stretches from right ankle to left ear, blotchily pink, raised like a low

Polynesian atoll out of the surrounding sea of skin. Trelawney is an unsightly mess and a light, restless sleeper. He and his wife keep to separate bedrooms. She won't eat off the same crockery as him and keeps her cutlery in her handbag, wrapped in a linen napkin. She removes her wedding ring and leaves it provocatively on the washbasin where, neglected, it gets spattered with soap and toothpaste. He doesn't dare clean it lest his actions offend.

Nothing is said about his mother. Or, to his relief, Mr Greene.

At first his wife leaves the house only to run an occasional errand, but by the end of the month she's absent for three or four days at a time. He doesn't dare ask where she goes or what it is she does. She's frosty and unapproachable; her make-up and clothes are an immaculate armour he cannot hope to penetrate.

The nurse swaddles Trelawney in loose bandages and sheets of lint and slicks his body with a heavy white ointment that smells strangely unmedicinal. He asks what it is. 'Vanishing cream,' she replies, and laughs; and from that moment, through a kind of sympathetic magic, everyone vanishes from his life: Abe, Lindy, his employers, his few friends, his colleagues, his wife, and eventually even his nurse whose elderly mother has broken a hip and requires her daughter's assistance. Trelawney declines the nursing agency's offer of a replacement. He turns the heating down low and pads round the house naked, enjoying the tingle of air on his skin. When hungry, he telephones for pizza.

Once again he's alone with his rash. Though of a less alarming hue, it stubbornly refuses to depart. But his wife will not be returning, of that he's certain: her clogged and smeary wedding ring has disappeared from the bathroom.

One day, strolling aimlessly in Soho, he suddenly catches sight of her. Not in person as such but on the cover of a magazine: *Leather Mistress*. She's wearing a full-face suede mask with pointed horns and not a damn thing else. Trelawney recognises her pale oatmeal skin, the taut geometry of her body, the sight of which momentarily dazzles and confuses him. He considers buying the magazine, but embarrassment obliges him to steal it instead.

Ineptly, alas. He's caught, and somehow the newspapers get wind of how he attacked the newsagent and beat him so badly he had to be hospitalised. They splash the story across their front pages, emphasising the kind of magazine he'd tried to steal. Sleaze sells, always has done, always will.

Shortly afterwards, a despatch rider arrives with a letter from his employers. It informs him, in the stilted chapter and verse of legal documentation, that, regrettably, his services are no longer required. A severance payment is enclosed; a hefty sum even by hefty sum standards. A proviso comes with it, of course: that the nature of his work shall remain, both today and forevermore, strictly – repeat, *strictly* – secret. That's the gist of it. He scans the document again and again, hoping to discover an error or an ambiguity, a hidden pocket of meaning, something personal, something that would allow him the option of returning it unsigned, to ask for a reprieve, to explain away his uncharacteristic behaviour, the difficulties that have laid him low.

There's nothing; it is flawless, impersonal, devoid of compassion. Trelawney sighs. He appends his signature and hands the document back to the messenger.

Flowers keep arriving by the vanload. Obviously his employers have forgotten to cancel the order.

His thoughts are madly scattered. He wonders what Gauguin would do in circumstances such as these. Buy a small Pacific island? Frolic in the surf, under an azure sky, with brown-skinned maidens? Marry a native woman and have children? Live on a diet of fish and fruit, on the beach, in a house made of saplings and palm fronds? Set up an easel and –

Unfortunately, Trelawney can't paint and, for what it's worth, public relations is his métier.

Briefly he considers setting up a roadside florist's stall with the blooms at his disposal.

Weeks pass. His life is in serious disarray. As his musings become darker, he sinks ever deeper into apathy and despair. Several times a day he contemplates the bright, potentially lethal knives in the kitchen drawer. But his pain threshold is extremely low (every one of his tattoos was done under a general anaesthetic) and he cannot, never could, stand the sight of blood, not even steak cooked medium-rare.

Repeatedly he dreams of standing at the foot of a

wall so high that the pattern of bricks and mortar blurs at the extremes of vision, inducing a kind of vertigo, a swoon, oblivion. Swooning into oblivion – that's how he wants to die. So, how best to achieve it? A quick Google search recommends hypothermia. It requires no elaborate preparations, no special apparatus, just a guaranteed overnight temperature of at least -5°C, his naked body exposed to the elements, and, to encourage rapid heat loss and bring about unconsciousness, whisky, half a bottle or so. But there's a snag: he hasn't got a garden. Perhaps he could die in someone else's garden, with the owner's permission, but more likely without. It would allow him a last look at the stars: an end to gladden the heart of even the most dejected Pharaoh. His mind is made up. But the leaves refuse to discolour and fall from the trees. An Indian summer prevails. People are walking round in shorts and skimpy tops. Acres of skin are exposed. While Trelawney waits impatiently for the days to shorten, for the first enticing frosts to appear, for winter's icy grip to be felt on the land, the detective agency's report arrives.

Their most significant finding is that Graham Greene is dead. His unpublished papers have been scrutinised by an agency operative, a moonlighting Literature Fellow from Gonville & Caius. Happily, the operative is able to report that Trelawney isn't mentioned in any of those documents. Furthermore, none of Mr Greene's characters, post-1985, published or unpublished, bear the slightest resemblance to him.

Finally, no letters have been found from Trelawney's wife to Mr Greene, nor is her name, married or maiden, to be found in his address book. That goes for his mother, too.

The agency has, on the other hand, secured – by nefarious means, one assumes, which even Trelawney feels obliged to tut about – a copy of his wife's medical notes. She's registered at a clinic in Southfield. He flips hurriedly through the pages. Is her address listed? Yes! Good! A telephone number, too. Nothing else is of interest; the usual childhood illnesses. But the most recent entry rocks Trelawney back on his heels. He can't – no, he can't quite believe it ... His wife is going to have a baby!

She's pregnant.

A mother-to-be.

The child is due soon.

Trelawney is going to be a father.

⊖

Here's how Trelawney makes sense of the situation:

While still at school, he accidentally impregnated his future wife inside a pantomime horse. This resulted in an unusually lengthy gestation. Soon she'll give birth to their first, and almost certainly only, child.

In a flurry of excitement he goes to his desk and writes her a long impassioned letter full of flowery rhetoric (which he knows she likes, though she pretends otherwise), and makes glancing references to Capri and gardenias (both of which, unequivocally, she likes). He describes the way light dapples the leaves of her favourite tree, the enormous elm on the street outside their living-room windows. He mentions the fact that – coincidentally? perhaps not – his skin condition, which disgusts her, and disgusts him too, has undergone a dramatic improvement. Already, he says, or rather writes, he can feel damage and disorder becoming an under-scab itch. Very soon, snake-like, he'll slough the outer layer of skin, tattoos and all, and hang it in the wardrobe as a reminder of his hidebound existence.

The memories come flooding back. He compliments her on her skills with the industrial power sander, the one they used to strip the floorboards in the hall, and he reminds her of how, when the boards were lightly stained, sealed and varnished, they sprinted from the kitchen and slid the entire length of the hallway in stockinged feet, laughing madly and – dare he suggest? – happily.

He reminds her of their epic snowball fight on Clapham Common, the violent flush it brought to her cheeks, her skin's translucence, the way her face shone like a surrogate moon.

Also, how he would lie awake in the early hours of the morning, watching her sleep, safe in his orbit.

How they ran naked into the sea on a moonless night, and all he could hear was the pounding surf and her yips and giggles and shouts of 'Au secours!

Au secours!' (they'd just finished watching a French film), as she successfully evaded his blundering and panic-stricken attempts to find her.

How, when drunk, they linked arms and he pretended to stagger, laying claim to her support, and she cursed him softly under her breath.

He mentions, in passing, the blissful mundanity of domestic life – shopping, peeling vegetables, putting the rubbish out in black bags – and invests such a wealth of poetry and personal feeling in it that he's overwhelmed by the absurd beauty he's summoned up.

He says that somehow he knows that's what she wants, too.

Then comes a particularly difficult moment. He takes a deep breath before renouncing, for all time, absolutely and irrevocably, Peggy Lee and all her works. Ripping up hundreds of her posters and signed publicity shots, he bundles them into the fireplace and applies a match. The paper curls, wisps and blackens in the flames; stray fragments rock and flutter a little way up the chimney before settling back among the embers. Such a rich and satisfying experience ... something he hadn't anticipated. He bags the ashes and bins them. He sends the few undamaged CDs in a taxi to Oxfam.

In an exaggeratedly loopy hand he tells his wife she'll make a wonderful mother, he knows she will. He also tells her that he carries, against all the odds, a torch for her – as plain and simple as that. Emotion lodges in his throat like a stone. And he forgives her for her drunken assault with the carving knife – not the assault that led to a charge of malicious wounding, dropped before it got to court because he refused to testify against her (and, in any case, wasn't it a breadknife on that occasion?), but the one that resulted in concussion (the knife nicked his arm and, fainting, he cracked his head on the corner of a coffee table); for, at various times, the bromides, sand, iron filings and laxatives in his tea; for the bleach and razor attack on his suits; for the occasional soiled tampon sandwich in his lunchbox; for the theft of his jewellery and the destruction of his alter ego (he's sure that was her handwriting on the burglar's note).

But from whom, he wonders, *did she obtain the semen?*

At length he forgives her for everything; even that. He forgives her for colluding with his mother in her relentless assault on his mental equilibrium, and as he imagines his mother reading this letter over his wife's shoulder, scowling habitually, he forgives her, too.

In the rapidly deepening twilight, Trelawney lights a candle and sets it down in a pool of hot wax. A thin plume of smoke rises waveringly from the flame. To cure it, he trims the wick with a pair of scissors that – no, that episode is also best forgotten. The flame increases; shadows recede; car headlights track along the walls and linger briefly in the corners of the room. Out of the corner of his eye, Trelawney contemplates his reflection in the mirror: bald, sallow-skinned but unwrinkled, ageless – and reversed, too, of course. But for once he *doesn't look* like an unhappy man; he has the potential for happiness somewhere within him. He's pregnant, in a way, just like his wife. The thought of it makes him laugh out loud. He imagines himself, his wife, his mother and Alex, little gender-less Alex (or Chris, or Lee), living together in harmony under the same roof; the basement converted to a granny flat; the nursery where Alex, surrounded by toys, romps happily in and out of an oblong patch of sunlight.

Yes, it's laughable; even while writing his wife's new address on an envelope, Trelawney is laughing and wiping away tears. Because his mouth is dry he sprinkles tears on the envelope flap, to moisten the gum.

An Interrogation

DO YOU RECALL the fateful moment when everyone's teeth turned to jelly, or was that just something in a movie I saw? Were you able to prise open the gigantic tub of Coca-Cola, big as a doll's house, using the miniature crowbar they provided? But why do that? *You thought something was swimming in it? In Coca-Cola?* Tell me, O Strange One, was housebreaking tacitly encouraged in your day? Did householders nobly submit to assault? Was life less sacred than a holy relic – the life of a freshwater fish, for example? Were you, as usual, kicking the gong around when the goldfish languorously began to lip-sync Billie Holiday singing *How High the Moon*? Was it just one goldfish or a vast shoal of Billie Holidays? Hold on, what's that funny smell, is something burning back there – I mean back in the days when cinema was young?

Did a religious sect, small but powerful (a word in the president's ear, etc.), believe that the dwindling sperm count in humans was attributable to eating fish, freshwater fish in particular? Would pumping cyanide into reservoirs, lakes and waterways be the best solution to the problem? Was the president deaf in his consultative ear? Is it true that the battery in his hearing aid was invariably flat, as flat as a pancake (or flatter) and kept that way on purpose by agents of the intelligence community? Was battery flatness the root cause of the president's paranoia ... and more: his Botox-suppressed nervous tic, his hysterical whinnying laugh, his epical bouts of depression? Does he believe that in terms of unalloyed genius he's Beethoven's true heir, though the only instrument he can play is the musical saw (and badly at that)? Is he keen to record – with the Berlin Philharmonic Orchestra, under the baton of, if he's available, Kim Jong-un (if not, Harvey Weinstein) – a tenor saw transcription of the maestro's Violin Concerto in D major, Op. 61? But what of his frayed nerves, are they equal to the task? Does he sometimes dream, as do we all, of running away from home to join the Mormons – or, failing that, the Taliban?

In which universe, remarkably similar to our own, did Beethoven compose *How High the Moon*? Is that also the universe in which chairs are a powerful aphrodisiac and propelling pencils are the root of all evil? Does the gravitational mass of the lunar orb tug at the blood in our veins, impeding its flow? Is moon-tugged blood reminiscent of the Danube as it glides powerfully through Vienna on its way to the Black Sea, or more akin to the lagoon-fed slap of the Grand Canal against staithes? Can simile piled upon simile sap our will to live? Are similes more dangerous than, for example, the boiling caldera that lies beneath

Jellystone Park; than paedophiles; than ebola? Do some renegade grammarians think similes are considerably more dangerous than metaphors and should be handled with care, especially the cold-blooded ones with muscular jaws and razor-sharp incisors? Is the president, as the news media has persistently insinuated, a closet freshwater croc fetishist? Is he? Really? How would one know if that were not so?

Are Creationists correct in their assumption that women have, at the base of the spine, a vestigial dinosaur brain that facilitates childbirth? Do they consider *The Flintstones in Viva Rock Vegas* to be historically accurate? Can their faith, as oft-stated, move mountains? Other than to prove a point, why would anyone wish to move a mountain? Because it's blocking the view of a scenic and extremely well-managed goods yard? But mountains are large and notoriously cumbersome; if you were given the task of moving one, how would you go about it? Wouldn't it be better just to shatter the mountain (this admittedly smaller than average mountain, hardly bigger than a hill, with a lone, stunted tree near the summit on which an eagle is perched) into chunks no bigger than your fist? Can faith do that, too? Can it sift the valuable minerals from those of little worth, commandeer the goods yard, load the ore onto a train, transport it to a refinery, sell it for cash and deposit the money in a newly opened, secretly held bank account in Grand Cayman? That parenthetical bird atop our hypothetical mountain ... doesn't it appear, when viewed through powerful binoculars, to be rather more vulture-like than eagle, and copper-clad, impervious to the elements, secured by large steel bolts to one of the limbs of a concrete facsimile pine? Can faith alone charm the birds from the trees and lure them into small-mesh nets? Is it, pound for pound, more effective than liposuction?

'Why,' wonders the child, 'has the moon grown increasingly distant? Is it because of the Earth's slackening spin, or has our interest waned during the long millennial dawdle?' What! – do my ears deceive me? Whose noxious tot is this? Should her precocity not be met with violence, as in the Golden Age? Wouldn't it be best to beat her with a shovel, chain her up in a dark, damp cellar for weeks on end and force her, as tradition dictates, to eat nothing but mouldy crusts, wood lice and rat droppings until scurvy makes her teeth fall out? No? Are we really not going to beat her senseless? Yet how, pray tell, can we avoid doing so? 'Wouldn't Amsterdam,' adds the whelp, thereby digging her grave a little deeper, 'benefit from having a mountain of its own, situated unobtrusively near the Reijksmuseum? And is it true,' she continues, 'that if there were seven men, each of whom was fluent in seventy-two languages (as many languages as there are in this world, according to the *Vercelli Homilies*), and if each of those seven men were granted eternal life, and if each one had seven heads and each head had seven tongues and each tongue spoke with an iron voice, still they wouldn't be able to enumerate the myriad torments of Hell? What's more,' says she, 'this thing about handbaskets ... is it possible to go to Hell in something other than one, or are the Hell-bound (myself included, perhaps, and sooner rather than later) obliged to use only that particular mode of transportation?'

Ah, but doesn't the saw sing beautifully as it bites into her chains, though it's a hacksaw of humble origin, little different in almost every particular from millions of its kind? Is its song an extraordinarily subtle, almost subliminal set of variations on *How High the Moon*, as one musicologist has hazarded, or is it what the proletariat thinks it is, a song of freedom, plain and true? Did the great Paul Robeson sound like this in his heyday? Psychotherapists tell us that prisoners everywhere dream the dream of the hacksaw, that it's a yearning dream of such potency they wake gasping for breath, in danger of drowning in a pillow saturated with their tears – but is this correct? Aren't the tears that prisoners shed exceedingly bitter, and famously so? As bitter as bitter almonds? Is toxicity perhaps even more of a problem than volume? Should systematic pillow drainage in jails be given more serious consideration than has hitherto been the case? Once the tears have been siphoned off, what then? Are they safe to be discharged harmlessly into reservoirs, lakes and waterways, or should they be harvested for use in biological weapons? But isn't the government's chief medical adviser concerned about something else entirely: the whereabouts of the president's lost equilibrium? Do his (the president's) tears frequently surpass in bitterness those of prisoners on death row, even prisoners innocent of the heinous crimes of which they've been convicted, child sex murders in particular?

As for phlogiston ... nowadays you never hear anything said about it, good or bad, now why is that? Were the phlogiston supplies completely exhausted, circa 1951, by the manufacturers of highly flammable nitrate film stock? Did the sheer volatility of nitrate film add to the excitement of early cinema? Were anarcho-syndicalist firebugs usually to blame, or could a single smouldering onscreen kiss cause a conflagration in the projection booth? Have you noticed, by the way, during outdoor screenings, how big the moon suddenly appears to be, how it hews close to the Earth and peers discreetly over your shoulder, eager to catch a glimpse of the action? What do you mean, *does the moon also read books*? How can anyone hope to read a book by the moon's meagre rays, light borrowed from the sun, reflected off the surface of an unpolished mirror? Ah, but of all the dust and debris satellites in our solar system, this one's different, isn't it? Don't we see something of ourselves in its cold, stony mass, something that fascinates yet makes us want to look away?

An Aristocratic Cure for Impotence, Languedoc, c. 1400

COLLECT UP ALL the silverware and hurl it into the moat.

Asylum

WE DO NOT have permission to approach the cabinet in which the syringes and surgical gloves are stored. We have been instructed to stand at least six feet from the wall on which the cabinet is located, behind a yellow half-moon painted on the floor, in serried ranks, breathing in unison like an enormous beast, an elephant perhaps. The room is hot with our closeness and foul, medicated breath and the windows vibrate to the tune of our despair. We are many, with the strength of few, and all too aware of our straitened circumstances – except, of course, for those who are not. The cabinet doors stand slightly, tantalisingly open, but all they reveal is a sliver of darkness. We can't see within, no matter how hard we crane our necks and how dangerously we lean over the yellow half-moon into the forbidden zone. Those in the second rank hook their fingers through the belt loops of those in the first to stop them toppling over. They say, 'What can you see? Tell us what you see.' Those ranked further back take up the refrain, somewhat plaintively, for their vantage is poor and they can have little idea of what's going on. Does the cabinet still contain what the worn labels say? The room is hot and the windows run with condensation. We yearn for the gloves and syringes, but they will never be ours, no matter how long we wait. We yearn because yearning is one of the few things we can do, for which permission has been granted. In truth, however, we've waited so long it's hard to recall precisely what our expectations were, or why those syringes and gloves meant so much to us.

⊖

Instead of the moss-green carpet, worn through in places to reveal an underlay of scuffed, plum-coloured linoleum, we try to imagine what moorland would look like if it were brought indoors, particularly into the lounge where we spend most of our waking hours, confused and/or agitated, uncomfortable in our skin and invariably bored, desultorily watching TV programmes about the world outside, the world in which our family and absent friends live, so many of them and in so many different situations, and we try to imagine being with them, zig-zagging through the throngs of shoppers on Oxford Street, perhaps occupying a tiny patch of sun-baked shingle on an otherwise crowded beach near Brighton's Palace Pier, or, by way of contrast, encountering a solitary walker on an isolated stretch of the high Northumbrian moors and sharing pleasantries, a flask of brandy-laced coffee and a sandwich, before going our separate ways, stumbling lightheadedly through the bracken while thick clouds descend and an icy rain starts to fall, which inevitably prompts us to imagine what it would be like if rain such as that fell indoors, on the bracken and our mossy carpet, on various weeds and half-smothered, ill-favoured saplings that surely won't survive the coming winter, even indoors, especially indoors, while we're desultorily watching TV, lying beneath bracken, almost completely hidden beneath a canopy of lacy fronds, wondering, as icy droplets fall at irregular intervals from the leaf tips onto our faces and roll down our necks, whether it's almost lunchtime, for flexing one's imagination is undeniably hungry work and if nothing else our basic needs must be met.

⊖

After the long-handled scalpel and the skull chisel have met on the mortuary slab and danced a stately pavanne with the toothed forceps, the rib cutters, the enterotome and the elderly bone saw's hyperactive grandchild, the Stryker saw, the next task is to wash and dress the corpse. On the windowsill: a hammer and a tin of nails. A coffin of raw pine stands in an alcove, propped against the wall. The previously autopsied residents gather round to assess the neatness of the job the pathologist has done, speaking so softly their voices barely ruffle the air. They inspect the Y-cut that begins at each shoulder and merges near the foot of the breastbone before travelling in a straight line from sternum to pubis. One resident remarks on how gently the upper flap of the Y was draped over the corpse's face, approximating the veil in which she was born all those years ago, in another century. There's a general murmur of approval.

The pathologist and his assistant remove their spattered smocks, bin their surgical gloves, and rinse the gloves' powdery residue from their hands. Deep in conversation about golf handicaps and property values, they hear the murmur, if they hear it at all, as wind in the trees, or as the distant thrum of washing machines as someone opens and closes the laundry room door.

Jets of cold water will buffet every inch of the corpse, rinsing blood and other bodily fluids along the slab's porcelain runnels and into the drain. Towels will roughen the skin but raise no colour. In the absence of mourners the coffin will be sealed – so says the pathologist as he and his assistant walk down the corridor, their footfalls and voices fading to silence. The residents are relieved to hear that the funeral director's beautician and her box of clown cosmetics will not be required. Happy, they disperse until once again summoned. All that remains is to dress the corpse in surrogate skin – a dazzling white shift which, for the moment, is draped over the back of a hardwood chair.

So beautiful is this tableau of shift and chair, in such softly waning light, it would be a pity to let it go unremarked.

⊖

Daily, to kill time between breakfast and lunch, those of us who aren't sedated take a long but far from leisurely walk. We stride down corridors past a succession of rooms: auditorium, kitchen, hairdressing salon, dining room, sick bay and snooker room, as well as day rooms, toilets, bathrooms, dorms and bedrooms, all of which we are permitted to enter though only at certain times. The offices, staffrooms, laundry and mortuary are forbidden zones, strictly off-limits to residents, and there are huge storage cupboards everywhere, rooms in themselves, most of them padlocked though they contain nothing more dangerous than paper towels. We walk swiftly, furiously, teetering on the brink of a run though we aren't actually allowed to run. Those of us who are devout offer a prayer to Mary, patroness of our establishment, which helps to boost our spirits and kill time. 'Sit mens sana in corpore sano,' the general manager is fond of quoting to visiting relatives and officials alike. Though untrue, as well he knows, it validates our daily walk, a troublesome activity he would love to prohibit but cannot; in their wisdom the hospital inspectors have deemed it healthful, and the clinicians, with minor caveats, agree.

Arms linked, closely ranked and sometimes twenty strong, we stream down endless corridors, staring into the distance as if in pursuit of a mirage. Cleaners swabbing the floor leap out of our way and press themselves against the walls, clutching their mops defensively. Their buckets of sudsy water we kick to one side. Gleefully flouting the general manager's ban, we race up several flights of stairs, panting in unison, and upon reaching the stairhead we dart like a school of fish to left or right. Whenever possible we act instinctively, without thought. This, too, kills time, bringing lunch ever nearer.

After maintaining this brisk pace for the best part of an hour, those who are less fit begin to ease themselves out of the pack. Without censure or regret we let them go. One by one they sink into armchairs in the lounge, gasping for breath, while a massive television set bathes their features in garish light. Now, with our forces depleted, we are vulnerable. The cleaners menace us in turn. Baring their teeth and making fierce, guttural sounds, they block our path, brandishing their mops like spears and swords. They charge, we flee, but try to make it seem less a rout, more a brilliantly staged strategic withdrawal. This happens every day and it fools no-one, not even fools. Abashed and weary, we meet for a debriefing in the studied calm of the snooker room. Beneath hot canopy lights, on a dazzle of green baize, coloured balls ricochet across the table and crash into each other, mimicking the early life of our solar system. No doubt there's a valuable lesson to be learned from all this. What is it?

Wooed

SHE COMPLAINS OF insomnia. I say: Is there any particular reason why you cannot sleep? Restlessness? Pain? Is something troubling you? The last question I ask reluctantly. I hope she will lie and say no. But it seems unlikely. Tonight's moon will be full; already it is buckling the rooftops, distorting telephone lines. Soon all communication with the outside world will be severed and the shenanigans will begin. Men will smear their faces with coal dust and rampage through the streets of the town. And this – this neurotic woman is only the first of my patients; the evening surgery has hardly begun.

She has waxy skin, a pinched, hollow-eyed look. I check her pulse, flatten her tongue and peer into her throat. I palpate various glands and place the diaphragm of the stethoscope on her scrawny chest. She flinches as the cold metal touches her skin.

'I'm burning, doctor,' she says.

'Hmn?'

'With love. Unrequited love.'

Had I heard correctly? I'm slightly deaf in one ear. It's either a chronic infection or an insect brood nestled within. But love? Unrequited love? There's something oddly and, yes, wearily familiar about that statement. I slide a forefinger under the lip of the desk until I find the buzzer, press it once, twice, then casually withdraw my hand. In the staff quarters, at the far end of the corridor, the alarm will have rung. Her demeanour murks the air like smoke. I go over to the window and open it a couple of inches. 'Stuffy,' I say by way of explanation, running a finger round the inside of my collar. *Where has Mrs Burridge got to!*

'So,' she continues, this intense young woman with deep-set eyes and midnight pallor, 'so you won't marry me after all.'

I've never seen her before. I'm the new doctor, she's my very first patient. I come from a town hundreds of miles away, on the far side of the mountains. What does she expect of me?

I force a laugh. 'You must be mistaking me for someone else. I'm married.' I reach across the desk and turn a gilt-framed photograph towards her: a woman and two children, formally posed, hatchet-faced and, I have to say, pug ugly – the local look. Had no-one thought to pack up my predecessor's effects and return them to his widow?

I jab the buzzer again, twice, and the janitor enters the room. Mrs Burridge arrives a couple of seconds later carrying a range of leather harnesses. She pushes past the janitor and dumps them on a table by my desk. The young woman fingers the cracked leather, the tarnished brass buckles, as though inspecting the merchandise in a saddlery. I draw a measure of sodium pentathol from a squat glass bottle and tap the shaft of the syringe with a fingernail, springing trapped air bubbles to the needle tip. While the janitor places his hands reassuringly on the patient's shoulders, I administer the shot.

I clear the desk and we lay her out. Mrs Burridge has forgotten the gag and goes out, tut-tutting, to fetch it. The janitor introduces himself. 'Henry's the name,' he says, and smiles foolishly, his lips a squiggle. We shake hands over the now semi-comatose patient. He demonstrates how the straps interlock, how tightly the buckles should be fastened. 'So you'll know in future.' His hands are large and very red, as though they've recently been boiled. Mrs Burridge returns with the gag, a semi-circular chock of wood padded with thick green felt. There are indentations in the wood that the felt partly disguises. Also saliva stains. It sits in my hand like a stick retrieved by a dog and I get a sudden urge to hurl it as far from me as possible. 'Really, I don't think we'll be needing this,' I say. Mrs Burridge shrugs.

Twilight is obviously notional at this time of year. In the blink of an eye the sun disappears behind jagged peaks. We are plunged into darkness, then the janitor switches on an electric light, the bulb dimmed by successive layers of nicotine. Tsk! – hopelessly inadequate. When the surgery has ended and the patients have gone home, I'll draw up a list of improvements. The blackwood panelling will have to be whitened, the cuspidor and ashtrays removed. So many ashtrays; they litter the table, the couch, the mantelpiece – every available surface. Was my predecessor a pipe smoker? Did he favour cigars handrolled on the silky inner thighs of young Cuban women? Out in the corridor voices are raised, sounds of a scuffle, people running. Mrs Burridge waves a hand towards the door and says, 'See to it, Henry.' She adjusts the straps, pulling them tighter. Henry goes out to investigate the rumpus.

I sit astride the woman, watching, while Mrs Burridge tugs violently at the buckles. I'm not sure what I should be doing. Doctoring is often like that, a practice riddled with uncertainty, but we soon learn to put a good face on it. When our training begins we are brash young men, full of puppydog energy and boundless self-esteem. This is entirely due to ignorance. As our learning increases the world expands and we, correspondingly, diminish; we shrivel and decay like a nut within its glossy shell. To our wives we are distant, we are cold to our children, but to our patients ... ah, to our patients we are the embodiment of wisdom, godlike in our power and reach. We can quell pain. Is it any wonder they fall in love with us?

The young woman moans. I shuffle backwards over her hips and thighs, trying to avoid touching her body with mine. A knee jerks up towards my groin, as far as the straps will allow, then gradually subsides. As Henry re-enters the room, Mrs Burridge unzips a sharkskin case and hands it to me. I open it like a prayer book in the palms of my hands. Scalpels; it

contains nothing but scalpels. Some, blunt and lus-
treless, appear to be antique. I withdraw one of the
instruments from its moulded groove and hold it up
to the light. When the patient sees it, her eyes widen.
She begins to struggle. She heaves up from the table
on her elbows, heels, the back of her head, thrusting
her body hard against the straps. She screams a guttural scream which sounds more like rage than panic.
Mrs Burridge hastily prepares a top-up dose of pentathol. And we apply the gag; there is, after all, no
sense in alarming the other patients.

Mrs Burridge administers the shot. As the woman's
muscles relax and her moans subside, the janitor rips
open the front of her blouse. Buttons pop and fly
across the room. 'Well,' Mrs Burridge demands, 'what
are you waiting for?'

That's a good question. What *am* I waiting for?
Guidance? Inspiration? Something along those lines.
Also, I have to admit, I'm shocked and dismayed. I'm
the doctor, a respectable, well-respected member of
the community. Why have I been addressed in such
an insolent manner and by a member of my own
staff?

The young woman's white satin shift is luminous
within the dark slit of her blouse. Mrs Burridge,
clearly exasperated, snatches the scalpel from my
hand, pinches the shift between thumb and forefinger, and makes a long vertical incision that ends
just below the umbilicus. But too deep, far too deep.
Henry obviously shares my misgivings:

'Mrs Burridge, do you really think –?'

'Be quiet, Henry.'

'But Mrs Burridge, I –'

'Henry! That's enough!'

Yes, just as I feared, the blade has passed clean through the shift and lightly scored the patient's skin. The edges of the cloth are beginning to darken with blood. The janitor is extremely unhappy about this turn of events; he hovers near my shoulder, wringing his hands. 'It's my daughter, doctor,' he says, his voice tremulous with emotion, 'my own dear little girl.' I look carefully; there's not the slightest family resemblance.

I hand the scalpel to Mrs Burridge and turn to face him. 'The wound will need to be stanched,' I say. But I do nothing. Mrs Burridge cleans the scalpel in a fold of her skirt and reinserts it in the case. As she melts into the shadows on the far side of the room, she says, witheringly, 'Well you're the doctor.'

Yes, I'm the doctor, the only doctor for fifty miles or more, and my responsibilities as such are onerous, grave. As a second opinion is a luxury I cannot afford, there's no option but to proceed.

I remove my jacket, roll up my shirt sleeves, and thrust my fingers into the gape of the patient's blouse. Her shift is slick with blood, its cut edges heavy and caressing. My fingers seem to go in a long, long way. I carry out the examination mostly by touch – moonlight is brighter than this feeble bulb. A lone dog howls in the street and others, near and far, take up the call. Tourists will be returning to their hotels in observance of the curfew. Soon the revels will commence, the long, grey, purgatorial winter will begin, and my work will be fraught with difficulties never hinted at in medical school, alas.

But in this case the wound is trivial, hardly more than a scratch.

The janitor sits, head in hands, groaning. 'Look,' I say, 'take a look for yourself. Not even a suture is required. Your daughter is going to be fine.'

'Godchild.'

'What?'

'Goddaughter. I haven't seen her for many a year. She was only a tot, but I'd recognise her anywhere.'

'For Heaven's sake, man!'

Despite my exasperation I allow him to inspect his goddaughter's wound. Joy suffuses his ravaged features. He laughs and claps his hands like a simpleton. He steps back half a pace, and I slide my fingers into a curiously dark hollow an inch or two from the patient's navel. Immediately I realise that something is wrong. I can feel muscle tissue, the firm rectus abdominis of a healthy young woman, but the muscle has been severed, sliced clean through, and bulging beneath it is the soft, slithery pulp of the small intestine. How can this have occurred? I'm up to my wrists in her abdominal cavity. The blood is flowing freely, the desk is awash with it – how could I have failed to notice? As I attempt to withdraw through the narrow slit in the muscle wall, something coarse and angular slides between my palms – a foreign body, something that shouldn't be there. Using my hands as forceps, I gradually tease it into the light, turn it this way and that, astonished by what I've found: an envelope, blood-soaked and leaden. I hand it to Mrs Burridge. Presumably it was tucked into the young woman's blouse and slid into the wound, this suddenly gaping wound – my trousers are soaked with its dark exudations. Mrs Burridge passes the envelope to Henry and assists with my attempts at resuscitation. Too late: she has lost far too much blood; she cannot possibly survive. I pound at her chest, force air into her lungs. She gasps, shudders once, expires.

Wearily I climb off the patient and slump into a chair. My first day on the job, my very first patient dead. Even before my certificates have been hung on the walls, my reputation is in tatters. I note with bitterness that my predecessor's certificates still have pride of place. What possessed me to venture across the mountains to this isolated town so different from my own? It is famous – notorious, even – for its nocturnal festivals and reverence for the dead. But I hadn't anticipated such a mortal blow, and so soon.

The janitor stands before me holding the sodden envelope. At a glance I can see that it has been opened. I have neither the will to take it from him nor the strength to refuse it.

'What is it, Henry?'

'A letter, doctor.'

'I can see that, man. What kind of letter?'

'A love letter.' His voice is pinched. I have the feeling that any minute now he'll break down and cry. 'A love letter, doctor, addressed to you.'

⊖

William, Dearest Will,

By the time you read this letter I will be dead. I'd like to think that my opening sentence will cause you to grieve for me rather than for yourself, but of that I cannot be certain. When your first car, an off-white Ford Escort with porous sills and 140,000 miles on the clock, seized up on the A23, and the mechanic (pursing his lips, as mechanics often do) said it was worth, if you were lucky, a tenner, scrap value, you wept. Rain was about to fall. You were fifty miles or so from home. You were hungry, thirsty, and utterly, utterly broke. Ah, how my poor heart ached for you. Elderly men cocooned in expensive automobiles swept by on the smooth black tarmac, and you sat under a dusty privet hedge and wept. I hope against hope you can find it in your heart to do as much for me.

Other than that I ask nothing of you. Marriage? A goad, that's all. To confirm my worst suspicions. If you acquiesced I'd probably spurn you. Self-abnegation has shaped the course of my life: I deny myself happiness because I don't expect happiness, and I don't expect happiness because I don't deserve it.

This is something you probably won't understand. But you are a naïve and foolish man, Will, and in certain respects you're hardly more than a boy. Let me explain.

When, as an eight-year-old, I gave up skipping and gave my rope with its intricately carved, pearl-inlaid handles to a child half my age, her joy was infectious. Despite my sorrow, I had to smile. 'Thank you, miss,' she said, and ran off, fat pigtails bouncing on her shoulders.

An exceedingly ugly child, as so many of us are. I felt sorry for her.

Father had recently insured the skipping rope for £50 – a considerable sum of money in those days – because it had an illustrious pedigree. In 1744 or thereabouts it was given to George III, who was, as yet, ruler of nothing but his passions. It then gave pleasure to several generations of royal infants. Eventually, scuffed and battered, it was consigned to a travelling trunk in one of the attics at Balmoral. But that wasn't the end of the story. At Victoria's instigation the skipping rope was refurbished and Edward VII was the last British monarch to use it.

The rope then disappeared for more than half a century.

It resurfaced in a private collection of royal memorabilia in Minsk, shortly after the Bolsheviks murdered Nicholas II and his family. Apparently it had been stolen from the Romanov household at about the same time. But the collector, a merchant, fell foul of the Bolsheviks and was obliged to flee for his life, shipping out on a freighter from Arkhangelsk. He secured his passage by bartering a number of items that had precipitated his downfall. The captain, befitting his status and the considerable risk he was taking by offering the fugitive safe passage, appropriated everything that had gold in it. The remaining items were tossed to the crew like scraps to dogs, and in the mad scramble for booty my grandfather, the ship's mate, emerged from the scrum with one end of the skipping rope in his hands. He tugged until the other end shot out from under the flailing mass of bodies on the deck, cursed his luck, stowed the rope in his kitbag, and promptly forgot all about it. Months later, when the voyage had ended, he gave the rope to my father. Father skipped happily with it, and I, in turn, skipped too, though less energetically, for by then its provenance had been established.

When I gave the skipping rope away, my father had been dead for less than a week. I was in mourning, bereft of my senses. Perhaps it's true to say that I never fully regained them. I relinquished my grip on the past to drift uninterruptedly, without oars or compass, on an undulating stream of time. I lived entirely in the present like a stone or a flower. But by the same token I was, of course, giving up on potential happiness. From the moment the skipping rope left my hand, it was obvious I'd never marry or have children; my life would be as circumscribed and dreary as that of an anchorite.

So, my dear Will, when I step into your surgery today I know what to expect. When I tax you about marriage, I'll enact my role with the charmless vigour of a minor character in a soap opera.

Finally I shall meet you in the flesh, my nemesis.

But you really mustn't reproach yourself for my death. If this letter conveys only a single sentiment beyond that of my love for you, it's this: you are absolved of blame. I don't forgive you – there's nothing to forgive. And I've taken the precaution of writing as such to the chief of police. You will, I'm sure, find him a sympathetic listener and, firmly opposed as he is to both corporal and capital punishment, a man considerably less brutal than most of his colleagues. He's also one of my uncles, on the maternal side, and I've been assured that he was a tender-hearted and loving boy and never – despite the times he returned home wild-eyed and dishevelled in the middle of the night, reeking of paraffin and char – an arsonist.

But that's beside the point. What do a few youthful indiscretions matter anyway? Were you yourself not prosecuted for urinating in a public place? Perhaps you don't remember the occasion. Or choose not to – I wouldn't blame you. You stood shamefaced in the dock. Already you'd set your heart on becoming a doctor and knew that a criminal record could ruin your chance of getting into medical school. Cystitis had made a seething cauldron of your bladder. So what did you do? You clambered onto the bonnet

*of a Volvo and urinated into a litter bin, under a
street lamp, right outside the Masonic Temple, and
at the worst possible moment – as the Chief of Police
was making his exit.*

*Twelve offences of a similar nature were taken
into account.*

*In mitigation it was revealed that you were suffer-
ing from stress: your dog, Schweitzer, was stricken
with cancer; you were bullied at school; you'd made
too many wrong deliveries and been sacked from
your paper round. The bedwetting that persisted into
your late teens should have alerted your GP to the
fact that something was wrong. But he knew nothing
about it. Nor even, for that matter, did your parents.
As a highly sensitive and secretive young man, you
preferred to launder your sodden bedding at 4.30am
rather than admit to such an embarrassing problem.
Perhaps that was what drew you to make urology
your specialism.*

*This lethal cocktail of frailty, stubbornness and
deeply flawed judgement was what drew me to you,
my nemesis. At first I pitied you, no more than that.
But in my eleventh year I developed pale and tender
breasts and grew inexplicably troubled. Night after
night I lay awake, thinking occasionally of you,
then, after a while, thinking only of you. And when
finally I slept, you strode purposefully into my
dreams, pitchfork in hand, and began heaving bales
of straw into a rustic wagon beneath a blistering
Mediterranean sky, pausing occasionally to wipe the*

sweat from your brow with a muscular forearm, and drinking thirstily from a jug of ale that had been brought to you by a beautiful, charming and utterly besotted farmgirl – me!

(I lie: in every dream I was plain, a drab, as in life, and you showed no more interest in me than you would a fencepost.)

You are, I know, a city boy through and through, who prefers vitamin pills to vegetables, who suffers terribly from hayfever and is wary of farmyard animals, while I ... I'm a country girl with typically bad teeth, a slight squint, wild black hair and superstitious ways, as witchy, pagan and rainswept as a menhir. Yet deep in my heart, despite all our differences (perhaps even because of them), I knew we were meant for each other.

In keeping with the custom for girls in this region, I studied the humanities at university and witchcraft during the holidays. I wrote essays on Socrates, Leonardo da Vinci and Henry James. I carved amulets, brewed potions, cast runes and divined chicken innards – always, alas, without notable success. Every drop of my magic was devoted to you, to your gradual enchantment, and perhaps I was a little obsessive and neglected my studies. After graduating with only a third class degree, I became a tour guide at Delphi. Those were, I think, my darkest days. The oracle turned out to be a flatulent echo.

Disillusioned, I drifted from country to country, bad job to worse, and only one thing kept me going

– you, dear Will, sweet oblivious Will. The mere thought of you was balm to my soul. Because of you I was able to pull myself together, return to the UK and sign up to a course in hotel management. It was a random but entirely fortuitous choice; I knew immediately that I'd found my niche in life, my métier. For once I was content, almost happy. I specialised in provisioning and dumbwaiter maintenance and for the past three weeks I've been the acting junior manager at the town's only four-star hotel, Hotel Excelsior, where you've been temporarily housed in the honeymoon suite until more suitable accommodation can be found.

Three times this week our paths have crossed: twice, in reception, I've lifted your room key from its little brass hook and handed it to you. On each of those occasions you maintained your natural reserve. But this morning I contrived a little clumsiness with the key, and as we bent down together to pick it up our fingers touched, our eyes met, and mine looked deeply into yours. My gaze lingered but you glanced away, embarrassed; you muttered something I didn't catch. There was no recognition. Not an inkling. Nor the faintest glimmer of interest. To you, I was a just a functionary. You didn't recognise me for who and what I am. And I noticed your eyes were green, not blue. I'd always imagined you with eyes the colour of blue glass marbles.

After you left the hotel I dashed up to your room, flung open the wardrobe and forced the locks on your travelling trunk. I thrust my nose deep into the armpits and crotch of your clothing. Nothing smelled right; it was as if you'd been caught in a flash flood and were obliged to wear garments provided by your rescuers. Your deodorant smelled of cardboard, your aftershave of liniment. The static electricity in your nylon shirts made them cling to me, drape themselves against my body, and I collapsed onto the bed in a flurry of tears. I was distraught, under-standably so, and took the rest of the day off work.

And what a long and painful day it has been. I've torn out fistfuls of hair and wept until I can weep no more. It's the disappointment that hurts most of all; my years of conjuration have been entirely in vain. All I wanted was for you to acknowledge me. But I know that when I step into your surgery this evening, you'll consider me just another ambulant sack of ailments. You won't even recognise me as being from the hotel.

And in certain respects you are – I must confess, even at the risk of offending you – also a disappoint-ment, less of a man than I thought you'd be, less handsome, less considerate, less intelligent, consid-erably less charming, and in all probability a bad physician (why else would you choose to practise in a rural backwater such as this?). Already your hair is thinning, running to grey, you have Victorian graveyard teeth, and yet ...

Should I fail to survive your clumsy ministra-tions, this letter will serve as my last will and testa-

ment, and as such I have a request to make, a request that even you, dear Will, surely cannot deny me.

It's a custom in this region that when a young woman dies, her fiancé assumes the role of chief pallbearer. I'd like you to do that for me: carry my coffin on your shoulder, rest your cheek against the polished wood, breathe a warm layer of droplets onto it and, as you bear my corpse to the graveyard through the crisp early morning air, tap out, in Morse code, on the coffin lid, as our customs also dictate (for we are a people who venerate custom), a few simple declarations of affection and grief, while a drummer boy beats out a tattoo to mask your lamentations. This will earn you the respect of our highly superstitious citizenry, who would otherwise eat dried cow dung rather than visit you in your chambers.

So, my dear Will, into your care I commit myself, happy in the knowledge that if my fate is sealed it will also inextricably be linked with yours.

Your ever loving

Lucia

⊖

What a weight the coffin is; it feels as though it has been lined with slate and filled with rubble. The pathologist is attending a conference in London, and his assistant is in bed with the flu, so perhaps I'm not mistaken about this. Perhaps the young woman's body is still in the mortuary, or been donated to medical students for dissection.

The streets are thronged with her grieving relatives, and that fiend, her uncle, the chief of police, is also a pallbearer; his hot breath frizzles the hairs on the back of my neck. He's confiscated my passport until his investigation is complete. 'We'll check with the police in your home town, Dr Mercer, to establish whether you are who you say you are and that everything is in order. It will take a week or so. I'm sure you understand.'

I hope and pray that my conviction is spent. If not, God only knows how he will use it against me.

In the meantime he dogs my footsteps. He arrives at the surgery unannounced, and with a wine glass held to his ear he monitors my consultations through the thin partition walls. He writes anonymous letters to himself, denouncing me. He sits in the hotel lobby behind a voluminous newspaper, smirking, wearing black spectacles without lenses, imagining himself hidden, peering through two eyeholes cut out of the front page.

And now he's breathing down my neck, compelling me to play my part in this absurd ritual. With one rap of the knuckle representing a dot, and a slap of the hand a dash, I must deliver a final message to the frumpy, hysterical young woman who perished in my surgery. '*I love you* will suffice,' he said, sliding a single sheet of paper across his desk: the alphabet and its Morse equivalent.

Thus, however reluctantly, the person wooed must become the wooer.

The drum clatters deafeningly alongside me and the pallbearers fall into step.

I love you indeed! It's ridiculous!

The cortège wends its way through the narrow, cobbled streets. Clouds hang low over the graveyard. Raising my hand above my head to shield my face from the press photographer elbowing his way through the ecstatic crowd of mourners, I begin to slap and knuckle the richly varnished wood.

Garden

ONE HOT SUMMER night, when windows have been flung open to capture the slightest hint of a breeze, the garden peers into the room, observes the humans clustered round the television set, and watches a programme about the Amazon rainforest, the jungles of Malaysia, Papua New Guinea, Burma and Madagascar, all the vast, gloriously untamed wildernesses scattered throughout the world, and hatches its secret plan.

Poultice

ACCORDING TO GRANDFATHER, every conceivable human need can be satisfied by the application of a poultice. He says the poultice isn't just a folk remedy made redundant by modern pharmaceuticals; new, improved poultices are being invented every day. If applied correctly, one of the most recent poultices, the ATM, can withdraw cash from even the most recalcitrant hole-in-the-wall machine, whether you're the proud holder of a bank account or not. The Nuclear poultice absorbs caesium 137 and shortens its thirty year half-life to less than a month. There's a poultice that, when liberally applied, removes God from the equation. Another greatly reduces the intensity of phantom limb pain. Yet another desalinates water. Recently, grandfather tried to interest the London Fire Brigade in an expansion foam version of a Sumerian Smother poultice, but his offer to demonstrate it was politely declined. There's even a poultice capable of defusing a bomb, if you can obtain the right ingredients and know how to make it, which apparently very few people do.

Grandfather has the recipe for that in his poultice book. The book is tucked high up on a shelf in his study, well away from prying eyes. But when he embarks on his evening stroll, I clamber up the book-case like a marmoset and sit hunched under the ceiling, snagging the ancient cobwebs that hang there like rotting hammocks, each containing the husk of a luck-less spider. With the book spread open in my lap, I marvel at the boundless ingenuity that has led to the Tooth Extraction poultice, the Lost Equilibrium poul-tice, and the so-called Recovered Memory poultice (popular with flaky psychotherapists and gullible hys-terics, according to grandfather's marginal note). Per-haps the earliest known poultice, the Perigee, draws the moon into a tighter orbit than usual around the Earth, though no-one seems to know what purpose this serves. Then there's the Love poultice and the Snake Charmer poultice, their recipes almost identical. But against all expectations, the Easy Birth poultice and the Accreta poultice (capable of detaching even the most stubborn postpartum placenta from its bed in the uterine wall) could hardly be more different. The latter resembles a wallpaper-stripping poultice called, for some obscure reason, the Trestle, which was used extensively in Hastings and St Leonards during the early years of the 20th century.

Of late, grandfather has been applying himself to the Sin-Eater, a poultice that has to be moulded to the male genitalia in the pouch of a dedicated cod-piece. A female version isn't imminent. As he con-cedes, some aspects of female anatomy have caused him no end of trouble. So getting at least the male version right is of paramount importance, not just to bolster his fragile ego but for the survival of life on Earth: 'If I can't create a workable poultice, humans will breed exponentially, without surcease, until each of us has only a square foot of earth to stand on and all other life forms will be trampled underfoot.'

He's begun to mutter about Judgement Day, prompted in part by his hellfire and damnation upbringing, but also by an unsettling letter he received recently from Professor Hans Schwoerer, a medical historian at the University of Bonn. Schwoerer had read an article, published in *The Lancet*, in which grandfather's reconstructed Malaria and Leprosy poultices were discussed. In a footnote, the authors mentioned that leprosy was once thought to be a manifestation of sin, and they made passing reference to the Sin-Eater poultice on which grandfather was known to be working.

Schwoerer argued that for the Sin-Eater to work it would have to be applied not to the genitals, as specified by grandfather, but to the cranium (perhaps built into the lining of a hat); moreover, because grandfather's conception of sin was extremely reductive, hence fatally flawed, his endeavours were as likely to succeed as the search in lost Atlantis for the remains of Noah's ark. In a rage, grandfather tore the letter to shreds.

This I saw from my vantage point under the ceiling, through a skein of dusty webs. Afterwards, to distract him, I asked numerous questions about his distant and, by his own admission, half-forgotten child-hood, when he too was fiercely inquisitive and as lim-ber as a marmoset.

Grandfather said he'd rather tell me about a dis-tant uncle of his, a Frenchman, who was placed under house arrest then driven into exile for having invented the Truffle Hound poultice, the recipe for which was destroyed to stop it from falling into the wrong hands. That, he said, was a prime example of Copernican dread, whereby innovation is suppressed or shunned by vested interests and the hidebound agents of orthodoxy. By, in other words, the Schwoer-ers of this world.

Also, his great-great-grandfather knew a man, an American apparently, who kept electricity in a bucket. A bucket with a lid. Of course, said grandfa-ther, that was in the early days, before anyone had trained it to run along wires.

A Valedictory Note

To my successor ...

It goes without saying that this is a great day for you. A plethora of medals, certificates and letters of commendation sing sweetly of your achievements. You aren't merely of the elite, you are now among the elite's very own elite. Congratulations!

But beware ...

Less successful colleagues will have observed your meteoric rise with envy and resentment – that's to be expected. As are the vile, largely unfounded rumours that are being circulated in an attempt to destroy your career. And, of course, the anonymous death threats. I'd advise you to take precautions. Check under your car with a long-handled mirror every morning. Have one of the more expendable juniors in the postroom gingerly open your mail. Don't eat more than once at any restaurant and never eat the same meal twice. Take different routes to and from home, and leave work and home at different times every day. Be extremely wary of edible gifts, even if you know the giver well, even if the giver is your wife or brother (the rumour that they've been sleeping together for years, and that your son is not your own, is probably false). Never drop your guard, not even while sleeping.

Most importantly, keep a loaded gun with its safety catch off in the following places: under your pillow (statutory); in the top drawer of your desk at home and the bottom drawer of your filing cabinet at work; in your tooled-leather shoulder holster, manufactured circa 1975 by Nudie's of Hollywood; under the spare wheel in the boot of your car; in the secret safe behind the hidden panel in what was formerly the dumb waiter in the dining room of your exquisitely furnished home; in an abandoned crow's nest in the high branches of a nearby copse; in the always mountainous fruit bowl on the kitchen table; at the bottom of your heated swimming pool, sealed in a waterproof bag; in various scooped-out books in your personal library.

The library will take quite a bit of organising, but it's well worth the effort. Here's how to go about it:

Shelve the books in alphabetical order according to author surname and make the first book of each letter of the alphabet your gun receptacle. Twenty-six firearms in one library may seem a little excessive but, trust me, one really can't be too careful. These are, as they say, 'interesting times'.

Now where was I? Oh yes ...

For additional security a handgun should also be deposited here or hereabouts: in the elephant foot umbrella stand in the hall; in the Vatican's holy time capsule that won't be opened until Christ's second coming; on a dry ledge behind the High Force waterfall in County Durham; in plain view, on a coffee table, disguised as a cigarette lighter (take up occasional smoking to legitimise its presence); in your best opera hat; in a safe deposit box deep in the vault of your Cayman Islands bank; in the Gaulby family mausoleum, the Outer Hebrides and the Xmas stocking of Sir Bernard Hogan-Howe, Commissioner of the Metropolitan Police. In other words, wherever you may be, or think you may be, at some future date.

Plan meticulously. They say you're never more than six feet from a rat, but if a handgun is always within arm's reach you can kill the rat stone dead.

As you are well aware, there's no limit to the number of rats you'll encounter in this line of business, many of whom initially look tame but soon prove otherwise. When you first entered the service I had you pegged as a tame rat, and, as you'll discover when you access your own personnel file (one of the perks of your new job), an utterly lame one, too. You'll see the file soon enough, but here's a taster – my preliminary appraisal, written on the day of your induction:

The calibre of the new recruits is, to say the least, disappointing, and Gaulby is the most disappointing of all. Having interviewed him this afternoon I'm at a loss to understand how he made it through the selection process. He lacks wit and wherewithal and seems to have no redeeming qualities. I suspect he would rank fairly high on the Autism Spectrum Quotient test, though his medical report gives no indication of problems of that kind. Best assign him nothing but grindingly tedious, nit-picky tasks of no significance whatsoever. The greater the drudgery and frustration he has to endure, the better. With a bit of luck he'll tender his resignation within six months. If not, we'll be obliged to ease him out.

Hardly a seer prediction, I'm sure you'll agree. I'd completely underestimated your staying power, and much else besides.

Later that week I summoned Jasperson – the officer who recruited you and other seeming no-hopers – to my office for a major dressing down. When I bawled him out he became distressed and cried like a toddler, knuckling reddened eyes, snot dribbling down his chin. This was unprecedented. Jasperson greatly admired the Stoics and was, in every respect, stoical. I'd never before seen him express an emotion. Yet here he was, sobbing uncontrollably. It was embarrassing. But to claim, as the coroner did, that this incident *gnawed away at him* and was, combined with an impossibly heavy workload and the culture of bullying endemic on my watch, *a major contributory factor in his decision to take his own life*, is absurd. Especially as the coroner's observations were based entirely on Jasperson's rambling,

semi-coherent and therefore wholly unreliable suicide note, which, regrettably, because of a lapse in
communication, we were unable to suppress.

I am, of course, aware that Jasperson groomed
you during your time at Oxford, and that you were, in
your own peculiar way, fond of him, perhaps inordinately so. At his wake you reportedly said he was 'like
a father to me, the father I never had', and according
to the operative's notes your eyes moistened as you
uttered those banal, treacly words.

Admittedly, the operative was watching you
through binoculars from several hundred yards away,
while perched halfway up a tree (a diseased elm, carefully chosen because it had a quantity of leaves sufficient to hide behind but not so many that they'd
obscure his view); but he had top quality Zeiss binoculars, 20/20 vision, and in those days his observational
and lip-reading skills were considered first class, so
there's no reason to doubt the veracity of his account
... In particular because (yes, why not admit it) I was
the operative in question, keeping my hand in, spending a few happy hours monitoring the behaviour of
the rookie who'd broken with protocol and requested
something inappropriate: compassionate leave.

Compassion we have none.

In this department the very word is abhorred.

Mrs Cooper-Bell was so taken aback that she author-
ised your leave without demur, though she notified me
immediately of this worrying development.

Those nearly-tears of yours were more worrying

still: an effete variation on Jasperson's theme of wholehearted, manly blubbing. I half expected to see you slump to the floor like a 19th century clergyman's wife faced with an unpalatable truth about her husband and a pretty housemaid. Everything I saw that day confirmed my initial impression: that you were temperamentally unfit for life in the service and would go to pieces under pressure. Although, to be fair, a colleague of ours, blessed in the department with the nickname Kenton Faecalmatter, said he thought you both sane and sound (qualities which he himself sorely lacked). He also said that talking to you was like talking to a waxwork dummy given voice by an I-Speak-Your-Weight machine – an observation I tender without prejudice or apology because it was, so I gather, meant to be a compliment. Ah, well.

Faecalmatter and I never agreed about anything, and about you we disagreed violently. We would be disagreeing to this day were it not for the fact that, as of last Friday, he is missing, presumed dead. The report is on my – I mean, of course, your – desk. There's nothing I can add to it but this: I am not responsible for Faecalmatter's disappearance.

Having deciphered a cryptic note pencilled in the margin of a street map of Bovey Tracey (where Faecalmatter's ex-wife now lives, and where, unless I'm mistaken, your holiday home is situated), I can only assume that Faecalmatter embarked on an unauthorised covert mission, the nature and purpose of which are (in a phrase so redolent of Victorian melodrama) cloaked in mystery. Perhaps we'll know more when we've reconstructed the shredded documents he left behind, thousands of pages-worth, enough for a taxidermist to stuff a zooful of animals.

I repeat: I am not responsible for his disappearance. Except perhaps inadvertently. A sin of omission. Let's leave it at that.

Ah, if only I could.

I suspect that if I don't take this opportunity to explain myself, my relationship with Faecalmatter will be misconstrued.

When I said that he and I disagreed violently, I meant the violence was not just, as per usual in our department, verbal; it was physical. He was a deeply jealous man and irrational with it. Although I'd met his wife on only one occasion, at a cocktail party (which you also attended; I'll say more about this later), during which she flirted mildly and somewhat tipsily with me, and I, somewhat tipsily, responded in kind (she was, after all, an attractive woman, a former Miss Swansea, or Swanage, twenty years his junior), he blamed me for the break-up of his marriage and tried to ambush me late one night in a poorly lit passage near Waterloo Station. As I passed a doorway that was deep in shadow, a length of lead pipe came whistling down. Faecalmatter was still a powerful man, but decades of chain-smoking unfiltered Turkish cigarettes had ravaged his lungs. Although it was a skull-crushing blow, intended to kill, it merely dented my bulletproof fedora, ramming it down over my eyes. Blinded and momentarily stunned, I fell to my knees, while Faecalmatter (for I knew immediately it was him – the distinctive wheeze in his chest was as good as a voiceprint) dropped the pipe, lolloped (his distinctive limp) wheezily down the alleyway and made, as they say, good his escape.

It took me several minutes to remove the hat, which was ruined and had to be replaced at great expense to the taxpayer.

After thinking it over, I decided against filing an official complaint. Instead I decided to shift the blame for the break-up of Faecalmatter's marriage from me to you. It was a partial success in that although I remained number one on Faecalmatter's hit list, you became number two.

After his first attempt to kill me, Faecalmatter and I continued as before, disagreeing about everything under the sun. But he knew that I knew what he'd done (or tried to do), and for a week or so he kept himself entirely to himself. He must, I assume, have been riddled with anxiety, wondering how I'd use this knowledge against him, wondering whether I'd retaliate and, if so, when; and quite honestly so was I. But in the end I did nothing. There was nothing I *could* do that seemed appropriate.

Once Faecalmatter realised he was off the hook, he grew brazen and contemptuous, more like his usual self (difficult, thoroughly dislikeable). Further attempts were made on my life – I won't bore you with all the details. But after the third or fourth such attempt, I realised he was in deadly earnest and wouldn't stop until he'd succeeded. He was, after all, obsessive, violent, narcissistic, delusional, manipulative and devious. In sum: a psychopath. Don't take my word for it, the annual psychological assessments in his personnel file make for interesting reading.

At work, Faecalmatter and I let off steam within the confines of my office, raging at one another, throwing things, occasionally coming to blows yet nearly always stepping out to lunch with several other colleagues, finishing each other's sentences and swapping feeble jokes, ostensibly the best of friends. It was a brilliant charade, utterly convincing; Gielgud and Guinness couldn't have done better. Actually we could hardly wait for the evenings and weekends, when, as mortal enemies, he would stalk and try to kill me and I would consistently thwart his plans.

Because he was an Olympic-grade marksman, most of his attempts involved guns. As the bullet sped towards me I would step aside, always at the last possible moment, and with a flourish guaranteed to elicit loud cheers from fans of the corrida I'd catch the bullet in a large, red, bulletproof handkerchief (as my grandfather, James 'Warlock' Wilson, stage magician, taught me), for I was nothing if not provocative.

Faecalmatter and I were playing a dangerous game, a game of cat and mouse, Tom and Jerry style, in which I, the wily mouse, always managed to come out on top.

(Perhaps I'm more of a rat than a mouse, who knows. But I think you know.)

I was, of course, aware that at some point Faecal-matter would have to be stopped; he wouldn't quit voluntarily. In the meantime I was enjoying his murder scenarios, enjoying them rather too much, perhaps. The thrill of anticipation was greater than anything I'd experienced since an unforgettable Xmas eve in early childhood, lying abed in a moon-lit room, the covers pulled right up to my chin, so excited by the prospect of what Santa might bring that I was unable to sleep, yet so exhausted that I began to hallucinate a thousand presents.

This was, as I would discover some years later, better than sex (as indeed most things are), better even than the thought of perfect sex.

Thoughts of perfection can lead us badly astray.

I had, for example, thought that Faecalmatter's murder scenarios were perfectly under my control. A mistake, I see now, despite the fact that, unbeknown to him, I had spies everywhere reporting on his movements. Bugs had been placed in his home and other frequent haunts, such as Claridge's Reading Room, his solicitor's office (the firm of Ceratogaulus, Spelaeomys and Josephoartigasia-Monesi, of whom Spelaeomys, a golfing associate of Faecalmatter's, had handled his acrimonious divorce), and the Knightsbridge pied-à-terre leased in the name of his on/off girlfriend, Daisy Bathurst.

As he swept his office regularly for bugs, there was no point planting one there.

An innovation that yielded surprisingly good

results was the bugging of his recreational equipment: golf clubs, skis, surfboard and vaulting pole, the last three of which he used rarely, the very last being used, as far as I can tell, only to dislodge his next door neighbour's cat from the beech tree in his back garden. (The tree itself was bugged, of course.)

Six agents and three transcribers were assigned exclusively to the case, the former working shifts 24/7. In total, almost one hundred bugs were planted. One bug, a faulty tracker no bigger than a sunflower seed, was inserted under the skin between Faecalmatter's shoulder blades while he was attending a Harley Street clinic to have a weeping mole removed. When the biopsy results came back, they revealed that the mole was malignant, as were several others. Faecalmatter had advanced melanoma that had metastasised to the bones of his upper spine and skull. At the time of his disappearance he had but a few months to live.

Surveillance as extensive as this is a costly business, but even if it cost me my job, which it almost certainly did, it was worth every penny. When alone, Faecalmatter was a profound, unselfconscious mutterer, unwittingly revealing his plans and incriminating himself in all manner of ways. There is, for example, good reason to believe that during the early 1990s he forwarded top secret memos to the apartheid government in South Africa; and, of even greater importance, he had something to do with Jasperson's suicide – or should that be 'suicide'? I urge you to continue the task of transcribing the golf club recordings, cost notwithstanding. It's a matter of national security, and moreover you owe it to Jasperson.

There is, of course, the possibility that Faecalmatter was leading us a merry dance with his self-incriminatory mutterings, taunting us with plausible nonsense. Only time and further investigation will tell.

But I knew something was wrong with him even before I'd received the medical report detailing the nature and extent of his cancer. Here's how. A shot he'd fired had missed me by three feet or more. There was a light, steady breeze from the south-west that day, good visibility, and I was standing perfectly still and poised with my back arched, chin thrust forward and tilted up, buttocks clenched, chest puffed out, right arm glued to my hip – a textbook matador stance. The conditions could hardly have been better. Without making Faecalmatter aware that I knew of his precise location, I turned towards him and held the bulletproof handkerchief up to my face. I knew its redness would stand out strongly against the white of my shirt. To aid him even further, I paused, as though awaiting a ripening sneeze. The wind tugged at the handkerchief, providing vital info as to how much lateral compensation would be required to perfect the shot. In such circumstances a marksman of his calibre would rarely miss, and never by such a wide margin.

On reading the report I understood why his aim was so bad: the cancer had spread to one of his eye sockets. Pressure on the eyeball had caused a slight but significant amount of visual distortion.

This was a dangerous development. If I couldn't rely on his superb marksmanship, I might, instead of stepping with stylised grace out of the path of a bullet, mistakenly step into it.

But, surprising though it may seem, death by misadventure wasn't my foremost concern.

In recent months the level of threat from international terrorism has risen from substantial (an attack is a strong possibility), through severe (an attack is highly likely), to critical (an attack is expected imminently). So far so good. The population is being kept in a state of perpetual fearfulness, their anxieties heightened by dire warnings of indiscriminate mass murder by what sociologists term the 'alien other' – in this case, Allah-addled nihilists who abhor the British way of life and want to kill us en masse for what we are not – that is, Allah-addled nihilists. My brief, endorsed by the Prime Minister during a private meeting at Chequers, was to coordinate efforts to tip that fearfulness head over heels into a bottomless pit of paranoia. This, I duly confess, I failed to do. I allowed myself to be sidetracked by the Faecalmatter affair, which was, as it happens, a supreme example of paranoia writ large, at least on Faecalmatter's part. I should, of course, consider myself lucky to have survived his lethal ministrations. But because of the substantial amount of time I had to devote to thinking about saving my skin, and even more time actually saving it, my departmental duties were sorely neglected.

And now, unfortunately, it's too late to make amends.

During an extremely terse conversation this morning with the PM's thuggish press secretary, I was ordered to stand down forthwith. 'Clear your desk,' he said, 'go straight home and stay indoors, curtains closed, until further notice. And for fuck's sake keep your trap shut!'

The resignation letter he'd prepared on my behalf, which you will have seen and on which the vultures in the news media will feast later today, mentions an unspecified illness and 'wanting to spend more time with my family' – an idea so appalling it almost made me laugh. I have no family to speak of other than a depressive, overweight, profligate younger sister whom I support financially but heartily dislike, and who, in equal or even greater measure, dislikes me. Gloatypuss is her middle name – which of course it isn't, but it should be. She'll chuckle mirthlessly at the news of my downfall until she reads the bit about me spending more time with her. O how I'd love to see her evil little face collapse in prunelike distress. To hear the weeping, wailing and gnashing of teeth (actually ill-fitting dentures, more suitable for a horse) would be better still. If only I'd had the foresight to bug her cottage.

As I began to write this note, two security guards entered my office and stationed themselves at either side of the door, arms folded, as stony-faced as the moai on Easter Island. Ostensibly they're here to help me carry a few personal belongings (pitifully meagre belongings, now I see them boxed up – is that really all I amount to?) down to Level 6 and the executive bay in which my car is parked, but their actual task is to escort me from the premises, making sure I leave without fuss and steal nothing of value. One of them has started to unscrew the brass nameplate from my door. The electric screwdriver he's using, hardly bigger than a propelling pencil, buzzes like an angry wasp. George – I think his name is George. He looks like a George, based on the Georges I've known.

'George ...' I say.

'It's Robert, sir. As you may recall, you attended my son Timothy's christening at St Giles, November before last, and were kind enough to agree to be his godfather.'

'Quite. Erm ... I'd ask you how the boy is doing, but as you'll no doubt appreciate there are a hundred urgent matters that require my attention.'

'He's dead, sir.'

'*What ...* ?'

'I emailed you, sir. About the funeral. Kath and I were sorry you weren't able to attend. I hope you don't mind me saying, sir, but you look a bit peaky.'

I have only a vague recollection of this man, his wife and child, their tragic circumstances. But it's true, I feel distinctly unwell. My head feels like it's packed with cotton wool that has been soaked in nitroglycerin. Prickly rivulets of sweat are spreading in my groin and armpits. There was something I wished to ask George – that is, Robert – but now, frustratingly, it's gone. The moment has passed, an opportunity missed.

'Any news of Faecalmatter?' I say.

That wasn't it, the question on the tip of my tongue, the answer to which he was bound to know. Everyone seems to know everyone else's business in this department, it leaks like the proverbial sieve. The Iranian, Sudanese, Iraqi, Afghan, Yemeni and Syrian cleaners (illegals all, I should imagine, as there seem to be no legal migrants or British subjects willing to do this kind of work) have access to more classified information than the PM has ever dreamt of; as has the departmental mouser, a fierce ginger tabby by the name of Morpheus.

'Faecalmatter?' Robert looks puzzled.

'Ferguson, his alias.'

'Oh, Ferguson.' He and his moai colleague exchange brief glances, imperceptible to the untrained eye. In other, less fraught circumstances I'd call them insignificant. 'No, sir, there's no news of Mr Ferguson, sir.'

'Has his office been searched thoroughly?' Perhaps this was the question I'd been meaning to ask. It's an effective question, in that both guards now look puzzled.

'I'm sorry, sir,' says Robert's colleague, 'but … could you remind us of Mr Ferguson's office number. Just to make sure we've searched everywhere.'

This is exasperating. I feel a violent rush of blood to the head. '439C!' I bellow. It sounds, to my ears, loud enough to shatter windows or start an avalanche on the flank of a distant mountain, but I'm the one who's shocked, the guards seem unperturbed. Never shout at minions is one of the golden rules of management, a rule I've now broken for the second time in my career (Jasperson being the first). The tension must be getting to me. With an effort I moderate volume and tone and try not to let the guards see how upset I am.

'439C is,' I say, 'as you'll doubtless recall, entered via the walk-in stationery cupboard 439A, in the rear left-hand corner of which, at knee height, is a dummy two-gang three-pin power socket. When a coded plug is inserted into the right-hand side, and the switch on the left is depressed, a sliding panel unlocks permitting access to 439B, less a room than a glorified corridor.' (My attempt to have it redesignated as such failed miserably, the estates manager being one of Faecalmatter's golfing buddies.) 'At the far end of the corridor, adjacent to a bricked-up window, is Ferguson's office, 439C, the key to which he leaves under the welcome mat in what could be deemed a postmodern or ironic manner, but as Faecalmatter wasn't by any stretch of the imagination a modern man (capable of changing a baby's nappy, for example), never mind postmodern, and irony was beyond him, I suspect it can be put down to nothing but carelessness.'

While I was relaying this information, Robert began to eye up the room chart on the back of the door. 'Are you sure about the numbering, sir? According to this' – he taps the chart with the tip of his screwdriver – 'the rooms on the fourth floor stop at 38.'

I know that 439A, B and C exist, despite what the chart says. Faecalmatter's office is precisely where I've said it is. I've visited it on many occasions, though always when Faecalmatter was absent.

Having said that, I'm not entirely sure he *was* absent, not always. Faecalmatter was a master of disguise and an authority on the art of camouflage. In one of his special training sessions with new recruits, he'd hide somewhere in the building, disguised as a desk, a photocopier, a coat rack or suchlike, and the recruits would be tasked with finding him. Simple enough? You'd have thought so. But invariably, after spending an entire day scouring the premises from top to bottom, they'd be forced to admit defeat, though not always with good grace. After several hours of mounting frustration, one hot-headed young pup ran the length of a corridor and punched a drinks vending machine, convinced that it was Faecalmatter in disguise. Only a chuckle from the water cooler right next to it gave the game away.

Then something occurred to me, an itch that had to be scratched.

'Bob ...'

'Robert, if you please, sir.'

'Quite. Erm ... Think back, erm, Robert. I believe you were the one who discovered Jasperson's body. Is that correct?'

'Yes, sir. We'd been asked to help with an audit of computer peripherals, Winston' – he nods towards his colleague – 'and me. We were opening up locked rooms so the auditors could audit the equipment. Mr Jasperson's office was among those that needed unlocking. He hadn't been seen in the building for several days. On the previous Thursday, just before lunchtime, his electronic pass had logged him in, but there was no corresponding log out. It was assumed to be a software glitch – we'd been experiencing problems for more than a fortnight during the switch-over from the Hicks system to Stanley. As you'll recall, sir, for some reason Stanley couldn't always read the Hicks chips in the first generation of security passes. Nor the second, for that matter. It was hard to keep tabs on who was where.'

'Yes, yes, of course. But … Jasperson's body. What made you think that a grenade had been lodged in his, erm –'

'Fundament, sir. Easy. There was a short length of fishing line wrapped several times around Mr Jasperson's right hand, and tied to the other end of it was a ring and split pin. The safety pin, it's called. Very distinctive. I saw immediately that it came from an M26A2 fragmentation grenade. I'd handled them thousands of times in the army stores. There was nothing in the cupboard apart from Mr Jasperson, naked, hanging by his neck, and directly beneath him was the pin. Gave me quite a start when I opened the cupboard door, I don't mind telling you, and the young lady auditor fainted dead away. So I knew a grenade had been primed, though for some reason it hadn't exploded. After searching the room thoroughly, the only place it could possibly be was inside Mr Jasperson. Process of elimination, sir, if you see what I mean. Luckily for us, the barrel diameter of the M26A2 is larger than that of the earlier model, the M26A1, and after the pin had been removed the muscular wall of Mr Jasperson's lower bowel and – pardon my French – rectum kept the grenade in place and the striker lever pressed against it. If the lever had detached, well ...'

'Robert, tell me this. Could Jasperson have removed the pin on his own, using the method indicated?'

'No, sir – absolutely not!'

'Because ...?'

'Because almost 30lbs of pulling power is needed to withdraw the pin from the grenade, and the fishing line was obviously of such low breaking strain it wouldn't have landed an anchovy without risk of snapping. I could tell that at a glance. Frankly, sir, between you, me and Winston here, I was surprised the coroner didn't notice. Not an angler, I suppose.'

A charitable interpretation of what happened at the inquest. (A travesty of an inquest, in my opinion.)

I've included these exchanges so you can see, and I hope appreciate, the skill with which this valuable kernel of information was teased from chaos, the chaos which permeates everything. The vagaries of our chaotic universe notwithstanding, I think we can safely conclude that Jasperson's death by hanging was staged. You and I know who staged it, though why he should have done so, I have no idea. That's for you to find out.

It will be nigh impossible to establish whether Jasperson's suicide note is authentic, given that the original has been 'temporarily mislaid' by the coroner's office. But the fact that the coroner, now deceased, was Faecalmatter's brother-in-law, must surely have had a bearing on how Jasperson's inquest was handled by the court. Perhaps, in this instance, the love between brothers-in-law carried a greater emotional charge than that of brotherly love, though Faecalmatter was about as loveable as a Portuguese man o' war. He was, however, as deadly as one, and a master of intimidation to boot, so fear may well have been the spur.

If I regret anything, it's that I encouraged him to believe that you and Mrs Faecalmatter were having a torrid affair. Not that my insinuations were needed; he had, after all, witnessed the passionate kiss that you and she engaged in, the kiss that followed on from mine. Sparks flew between the two of you and the temperature in the room shot up by several degrees. And when immediately after the divorce she moved into a property right next door to your holiday home, and a semi-detached one at that (you even share a driveway and your cars park nose to tail!), his worst suspicions must have been confirmed.

It was remiss of me to do that, given his 'craving

for barbaric splendour, for savagery and colour and the throb of drums', as Thesiger put it; and, of course, a propensity for vendetta. I think, in a distant Utopia of my mind, I rather enjoyed hearing your most vocal supporter's cheers turn to boos and hisses, and I was so wrapped up in my own business with Faecalmatter that I turned a blind eye to the likely consequences of my actions. But you will have dealt with the matter efficiently and effectively and, what's more, discreetly, as is your wont. Faecalmatter would have expected nothing less. I realise that I'll probably never get to know what became of him, but not a squeak will you hear from me. What curiosity famously did for the cat it could just as easily do to the rat. I wash my hands of the whole sordid affair, and with it my once brilliant career will gurgle down the drain.

It strikes me at this juncture that redundancy counselling might be beneficial, to smooth my painful transition from entity to nonentity. The counsellor would, of course, have to understand the particular and sometimes downright peculiar sensitivities of the intelligence community, which often defy logic and fly in the face of common sense and even common courtesy. For example, once I've become a persona non grata, former colleagues will be obliged to shun me in public. I'm aware that I must act as though the shunning isn't taking place, and that I, the person shunned, and, for example, Yodelman (not his real name; the alias of a friend and colleague), awkwardly cast in the role of shunner, have never met. Not a flicker of recognition must pass between us. We should try to be as neutral as water. Or Switzerland.

Easier said than done, of course.

'Beware of overshunning,' counselled my mentor, just a few weeks prior to his being dismissed and thereby shunned, the deep humiliation of which sent him scurrying, tail tucked between his legs, from Pimlico to a smallholding some ten miles north of Leamington Spa, never to be seen or heard from again. 'If the shun is too powerful it can create a zone of negative energy, drawing the attention of casual observers like iron filings to a magnet.'

Wise words. I'm indebted to him still. As, I hope, you will be to me.

Though quite what Yodelman and I are supposed to do when, of an evening, we sit side by side in our grand tier box at the Royal Opera House, I have no idea. What kind of space is it: public or private? If public, does it become private when the house lights go down and the orchestra strikes up? Can Yodelman and I then share bitter chocolate and a flask of black coffee laced with brandy, as we've always done, or must we develop incompatible tastes in opera so we never again risk attending the same performance? Perhaps, being unemployed, I could still favour Verdi and Puccini but switch to matinees only. Would that be a better solution?

These questions are, of course, purely rhetorical –

but guidance must be sought. If all else fails there's bound to be something pertinent in the Yanji Handbook, though locating the problem context within its unindexed 700+ pages will be absurdly difficult given that the print in the handbook is microscopic, readable only with the aid of a strong magnifying lens, and the book itself, of which there's but a single copy in circulation at any one time, is disguised as a voluminous series of footnotes and appendices to a legal agreement between a microchip manufacturer and a cellphone company. What's more, the handbook is shelved at a different location every day, according to a coded rota, and often deliberately misshelved by person or persons unknown. Were that not a sufficient level of difficulty, the handbook is written in a jumbled version of the two official languages of the Yanbian Korean Autonomous Prefecture, which three of our operatives are capable of translating though only one is stationed at Millbank and currently she's on maternity leave.

I would expand on this vexing topic, but time is tight. Robert and Winston are starting to fidget, and all this windy grumbling is keeping me from the substantive issue – your imminent arrival and my even more imminent departure.

You've been waiting patiently in the wings, an understudy who knows his lines and has the stagecraft and confidence to believe that, given a chance, he can trump his master, that patent old fraud. And perhaps you can, if past efforts are indicative of your potential.

I hand it to you: presenting the 'elimination' of three terrorist suspects at a semi-rural retreat in Derbyshire as a paintballing exercise between rival firms of pest controllers was a masterstroke.

Even when two of the suspects escaped to Matlock from the rear of the property and had to be taken down in Lilybank Close, you made it seem as though the paintballers had merely become a tad boisterous, having supped too much ale with their ploughman's lunch. The idea of having several of our operatives play dead, as dead-looking as the suspects actually were, was excellent. At a distance of five paces or more the blood was indistinguishable from paint; not even a top surgeon could have told the difference. The bodies, dead and acting dead (and by all accounts the latter were very convincing; those themed workshops with members of the Royal Shakespeare Company, obligatory for new recruits, have proved invaluable), were bundled into cars and sped away to a secret location. Within seconds the close was clear. It was a meticulously planned and executed operation, with strong contingency.

Assuming the guise of a freelance journalist, as you did, and offering the *Derbyshire Times* a 'drunken paintball pests invade Matlock' story (complete with doctored cellphone images and grovelling apologies from the managing directors of the paintball company and the two pest control firms), deflected awkward questions that might otherwise have arisen.

To top it all, the discreet word you had with the Chief Constable for Derbyshire stifled any possibility of a police investigation.

No detail too small, nothing overlooked.

That the first major operation under your command was an unqualified success would in itself have guaranteed your swift elevation through the ranks, but you then followed it up with a series of spectaculars (the name by which terrorists also refer to their explosive bouts of massacre and mayhem, as though terrorism were but a dystopian branch of the entertainment industry, which I suppose it is), all of which were carried out in secrecy so absolute (how on earth did you manage it?) that most of our colleagues, and the news media in toto, had no idea they'd taken place.

Faecalmatter shivered in ecstasy and went into raptures after each of these operations, praising you so outrageously that had the gods on Mt Olympus eavesdropped they'd have developed a crippling inferiority complex.

It was, quite frankly, nauseating, and it stoked white hot the furnace of my anger.

Whenever Faecalmatter and I argued about you, which was often, I played, so he thought, devil's advocate, but I did it with absolute conviction and spittle-flying intensity, channelling all the vitriol, rage and sulphurous scorn of Beelzebub himself. Red-faced, hot under the collar, with sour beads of sweat popping on my brow, I railed against you and everything you stood for, even the many things on which you and I would doubtless agree. But no matter how hard I tried, my arguments seemed blustery and hollow when set against your achievements, and Faecalmatter countered them effortlessly.

That wasn't the worst of it. What upset me most of all was his gloating. It got deep under my skin and dripped poison into my dreams.

Because of his provocations, and after months of disturbed sleep, my judgement may have become slightly skewed. It's the only explanation I can offer for something I did, something I probably shouldn't have done but which I don't, for one moment, regret: I signed the authorisation document for Trial by Tribulation – a procedure you may not have heard of, based loosely on the Book of Job, which we've employed only twice in the department within the last quarter century. There's good reason for its sparing use. On both occasions the person being tried had a catastrophic nervous breakdown and was invalided out of the service and placed in a care home, there to eke out his dying days.

Consult the Trial by Tribulation entry in the Yanji Handbook, if you can find it.

Trial by Tribulation, perhaps the most extreme test of mettle and loyalty ever invented, is designed to knock you off your feet and carry you helplessly, head over heels, on the forward wave of an avalanche, pummelled, bloodied and dazed, to the very brink of annihilation. Absolute secrecy is vital to its success. The person on trial, and everyone around him, must remain unaware that he is being tested. I knew your trial could only be kept secret in our leaky department by hiding the authorisation document in an unlikely place (wedged behind one of the lavatory cisterns in the executive washroom, where it remains to this day), telling no-one what I was up to (especially not Faecalmatter), and bringing in operatives who had no connection with the service – petty criminals, illegals, rough sleepers, etc. With their admittedly somewhat erratic help, things would be made to happen to you, unaccountable and incomprehensible things, always bad and sometimes truly terrible things, one after another after another after another without pause or relent, as though God had singled you out for cruel and unusual punishment.

When you'd become a gibbering, simian wreck – as surely you would, and in record time – such a pale shadow of your former self that you'd struggle to recognise your own face in a shaving mirror, here's what I'd say to Faecalmatter:

Take a long, hard look at your golden boy. That's what he amounts to, it's all he's ever amounted to – a quivering jelly and a bag of broken sticks!

Then it would be my turn to gloat, and gloat I most certainly would.

Inspired by this happy thought, I got to work. The partial collapse of the roof of your house, which was attributed to galloping dry rot; the near-fatal bout of clostridium difficile your father-in-law suffered when hospitalised with a broken femur after toppling from a ladder; the contents of your investment portfolio wine cellar, deep in a cave in the Italian alps, that overnight became vinegary sludge; the deaths, all within a matter of days, of the family dog, two cats, your son's goldfish and the occupants of an entire hen house, tough old roosters included; the crop of King Edwards you teased from the tilth of your vegetable patch, every spud spaded though no spade had been anywhere near them; the reckless newspaper editorial that mistakenly outed you as a paedophile and the mob of anti-paedophile hysterics that broke your windows, stuffed petrol-soaked rags through your letterbox and set them ablaze, overturned and wrecked your car, and forced you, your wife and son to flee by moonlight over the back fence and into an elderly neighbour's unkempt garden, there to cower in a thorn bush until a police helicopter found you and winched you to safety; the faulty satnav in the furniture van that caused all your worldly goods to be transported to a derelict building on the outskirts of Kingston upon Hull rather than your mini-mansion on the outskirts of Kingston upon Thames, from where (Hull) they were, in a trice, stolen; the parcels of excrement your wife received on a daily basis for several weeks thereafter, special delivery, with your brother's name and address on the return label; the false positive results and misleading scans that made hospital consultants think you had a deep brain tumour, resulting in invasive surgery and a shaved, sawn, superglued and crudely stitched skull that

looked like the work of a latter-day Victor Franken-
stein; the rogue seagulls that shat on your coat and
hat; the starlings, pigeons, wrens, magpies, sparrows,
crows, finches, robins, hawks, tits, owls and, extraordinarily, the large flocks of great bustards and little
bitterns that did likewise; the leaflet delivered to every
household in Kingston upon Thames entitled 'There's
a Cannibal in our Midst', which alleged that you regularly stole body parts from the local morgue for midnight fry-ups; the slab of frozen urine, 'accidentally'
voided from an incoming transatlantic jet, that landed
in your ornamental pond killing Hugo, your prize
carp; the Class A drugs the school found in your son's
lunchbox; the solitary drink you had after work, to
calm your frayed nerves, from which you awoke three
days later, in a ditch in Norfolk, with a male escort
agency's business card tattooed on your chest; the hail
of meteorites that flattened your greenhouse; the
thought-to-be-rabid bat that entered through a partly
open bedroom window and bit you in your sleep; the
ream of confessions to arson and gross sexual misconduct, written in your own hand, that were folded into
paper planes and launched from the roof of a multi-
storey car park; the blood tests that revealed you, your
wife and son were HIV Positive; the three coffins, one
smaller than the other two, left in your garage while
no-one was at home; the malfunctioning central heating boiler that exploded, wrecking your utility room;
the nuisance telephone caller, pursuing you from one
unlisted number to the next, who impersonated a host

of cartoon characters (Deputy Dawg, Bart Simpson, Popeye, Foghorn Leghorn, etc.) but limited himself to intoning, in an actorly manner, 'Now is the winter of your discontent'; the Icelandic bank that failed and the hedge fund that collapsed, wiping out your savings and investments; the ineradicable stench of the charnel house that seeped from the pores of your skin no matter how often you bathed; the piano string that broke while you were pounding out Henry Cowell's *Anger Dance*, one end of which whiplashed from the piano interior and wound itself like a garrotte round your neck, causing oxygen starvation and a near-death experience in which you met God, or a white-robed being purporting to be him, and without a word of explanation struck him full in the face ...

All of those things and many, many more were, I'm proud to say, my doing.

I wish I could also say I'd broken you. Nothing would give me greater pleasure. But despite the significant weaknesses that, unfathomably, I alone seem to have identified in your character, you managed to weather the Trial by Tribulation shit storm (a term frequently used by many of the younger agents – but what do you expect, they're a brash, vulgar lot, drawn mainly from red brick universities, sink estates and young offender institutions).

My uncharacteristic lurch into demotic speech is by way of acknowledging that you did indeed, as mentioned above, suffer an epical storm of excrement, a trial you survived relatively unscathed though your family wasn't spared. Your wife half-heartedly tried to commit suicide (a weepy, self-pitying phone call to the Samaritans, and a fistful of toxic pills washed down with a cracked cup of gin, do not a credible suicide attempt make); your son developed selective mutism (he'll speak to anyone but you – even rats, even, at a pinch, bacteria); your deceased carp Hugo has been immortalised in verse but, alas, bad verse, lacking the narrative thrust, lock-step metrics and clanging rhymes of a seasoned McGonagall; your father-in-law ... ah yes, your recently hale father-in-law, poor man, now comatose, at death's door, whose last lucid moments were spent cursing you for the loan of a wonky ladder ...

I could go on, but I won't. You know full well what has befallen you, in all its devilish diversity.

Do I hear aright – the massed but muffled clump-clump-clump of feet, marching ever closer, as you and your retinue sweep through the building at breakneck speed?

Perhaps it's just the blood pounding in my ears.

But I sense (the hair on my neck and arms standing erect) that you're nearby, perhaps in the office next door, which the doughty widow and former society beauty Arabella Cooper-Bell usually occupies. While I've been cramming my pitifully meagre belongings into a box no bigger than a baby's coffin, and penning this futile note – which you'll crumple, unread, and toss into the nearest wastepaper basket, or hold by one corner between thumb and forefinger, at arm's length, as if in disgust, while feeding it into a shredder – you've probably been sitting in her sumptuously upholstered chair, sullying her clean and immaculately tidy desk with your feet, twiddling your thumbs and sighing histrionically, wishing the old fool next door would for pity's sake, for fuck's sake, please, just get a bloody move on.

And so I shall, there's no need to nag.

'Stand not upon the order of your going, but go at once,' quoth Lady Macbeth, a little fraught. Of course, of course. If only it were that simple.

It would be hugely embarrassing for all concerned were you and I to bump into each other while I was being escorted from the building. I would, unsurprisingly, have nothing more to say to you, having said everything worth saying here. But as we passed one another, I'd hold my head high, and perhaps you'd lower yours, turning your face away, unable to meet my gaze, feeling ashamed, or perhaps just making a pretence of it. How would I tell the difference? Were your emotional response sincere, I'd perhaps detect a flush of colour at the nape of your neck, and I'd try to restrain myself from spinning round and slapping you hard in that quarter, raising an even greater flush and, if possible, knocking you to the ground. If insincere, I'd hold you in even greater contempt than I do already, and were there any justice in this world your testes would wither on the vine.

Status update: Robert's phone has just beeped distractingly. He flips it open, stares at the lit screen with massive concentration, then opens the door. A porter with a cellphone in one hand drops a grey polypropylene mail sack, large, empty, at Robert's feet and whispers a little something in his ear. Robert then whispers in Winston's ear. Before exiting, the porter glances in my direction and ... do I detect on his rubbery face the beginnings of a smirk, or was that barely detectable curl of the lip a grimace?

No matter. I know what the sack is for.

If I kick up a stink and refuse to go quietly, my wrists and ankles will be bound with duct tape, another strip of tape will be wound round my head several times, sealing all orifices apart from, I hope, my nostrils, and I'll be bundled into the sack and carried to Level 6 where my car awaits, its boot open.

Ours is still, in many respects, a civilised country. Were this to happen in one of the many despotic regimes our government officially condemns but secretly supports, an anchor would be placed in the sack with me, and my destination would be a watery grave rather than a cottage in Twickenham with roses and wisteria round the door.

'Are you ready, sir?'

Indeed I am not. Nor will I ever be, not until the sun dies, snuffing out life on Earth.

I counter his question with one of my own:

'Is there an anchor in the boot of my car, Robert?'

This catches him unawares, despite the fact that he knows I'm a nautical cove, a weekend sailor who circumnavigates the Isle of Wight in a beautifully restored Eikboom Folkboat called the *Margaretha Geertruida Zelle* (there's a framed photo of it on my desk – or rather in my takeaway box). He looks immediately ill at ease, as though a switch has been flicked. His muscles tense involuntarily, pulling his shoulders down, making him seem more squat than he actually is.

Perhaps he's been reminded of my surprise 60th birthday party, when a large cake, in the shape of an anchor, studded with lit candles, was wheeled into the packed canteen at twilight. He – yes, Robert, the very same, I'm sure it was him, or someone very much like him – brought the cake trolley to a halt in the middle of the room, where I'd been lured by Yodelman under false pretences. As the Red Sea obligingly parted for Moses and his harried gaggle of Israelites, so the hushed crowd had made way for Robert and my birthday cake. (Now that I think of it, this marked the point at which my very own exodus began, though not one that Moses would recognise – my journey into the post-employment wilderness, as inexorable in its progress as twilight shading into dusk.) It was a spellbinding moment, broken by a spontaneous round of applause, the draught from which blew several of the candles out.

But now's not the time for fond reminiscences, as Robert well knows.

'Should there be, sir?'

As he says this, Winston picks up some files set

aside for Mrs Cooper-Bell and drops them into the sack. He ties the neck of the sack tightly, doubles the knot, and places the sack in the corridor, leaving the door subtly ajar.

So, Twickenham, wisteria and roses it is. If traffic is light on the A316, I'll be home in time to catch the early evening news on TV, in which yours truly will feature unless an extravagantly-coiffed pop tart, her dress spattered with vomit, has slapped a photographer outside a nightclub at 4.00am, or an inarticulate premier league footballer has stubbed his toe, either of which would take priority in the schedule. And if I feature, so too, my dear Gaulby, must you, despite your ten unstubbed toes and laughably bad haircut (do you, as various colleagues have suggested, cut it yourself, in the dark, left-handedly, with pinking shears? – perhaps that's the fashion nowadays, I really wouldn't know).

Though for old times' sake I'd love to inflict a deep and lasting wound, I know from bitter experience that verbal barbs such as the one above will barely tickle your hide, never mind pierce it, and sticks and stones will fare no better.

So be it.

You've won.

Nothing remains for me now but to become a former spook, a shadowman. I'll skulk about in darkened rooms and view life through the chink in closed curtains. Black spot will devour the roses and the wisteria will die from neglect, what do I care? If my sister (who bears, now that I think of it, an uncanny resemble to Faecalmatter, down to the caterpillar eyebrows and scornful cupid lips) pays me a surprise visit, claiming to be worried about my state of mind but actually, as per usual, seeking a gladsome handout, perhaps I'll take the opportunity to strangle her and place her in the capacious chest freezer I bought for that purpose almost a decade ago. Best laid plans, eh? I'd arrange her body carefully like the stone effigy on a medieval tomb, in a mockery of prayerful repose, with my American Express Platinum card clasped between her palms (or thighs).

What then?

Then I would do what I longed to do as a child, but never did, for lack of courage: don a black frock coat, a black eye patch and a black tricorn hat, all with gold trim – the outfit I wore to our fancy dress party last Xmas but 'forgot' to return to the theatrical costumier – and become, to all intents and purposes, a swashbuckling pirate. I'd bin the plastic sword and scabbard, as supplied by the costumier, strap on my father's regimental sabre and take to the high seas.

I would, of course, revisit the house from time to time, always in the dead of night, principally to gloat over my sister's remains, her protruding tongue almost black, spotted with freezer burn, her bulging eyes filmed with cataracts of ice. That would put a spring in my step and a song in my heart, no doubt about it.

Returning to Portsmouth at the crack of dawn, I'd

hoist the Jolly Roger on the *Margaretha Geertruida Zelle* – a boat bristling with guns of all shapes and sizes (an arsenal of which the Royal Navy, facing yet another round of budget cuts, would justifiably be envious) – and spend my days sailing round the Isle of Wight, looking for the perfect spot to bury my 'treasure' (i.e., sister), the location of which I'd indicate, as pirates traditionally do, with a rather vague X on an equally vague map.

Also available from grand**IOTA**

APROPOS JIMMY INKLING
Brian Marley
978-1-874400-73-8   318pp

WILD METRICS
Ken Edwards
978-1-874400-74-5   244pp

BRONTE WILDE
Fanny Howe
978-1-874400-75-2   158pp

THE GREY AREA
Ken Edwards
978-1-874400-76-9   328pp

PLAY, A NOVEL
Alan Singer
978-1-874400-77-6   270pp

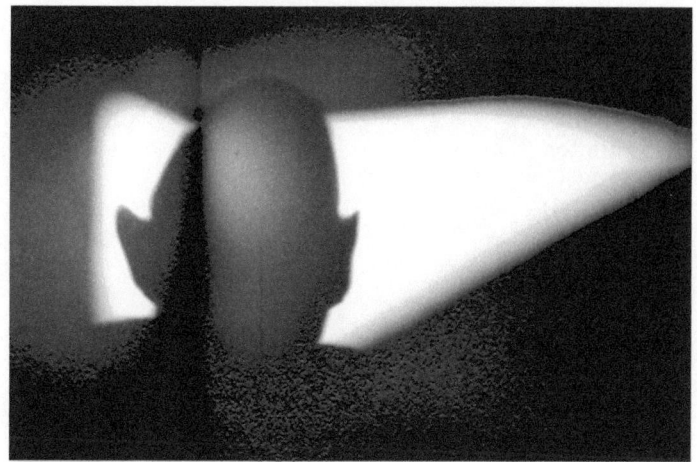

Brian Marley has published books of poetry, music criticism and fiction. His most recent publication is a novel, *Apropos Jimmy Inkling*, which reveals that when gangsterism meets showbiz the possibilities are limitless and all bets are off. A palimpsest novel, *Crime, My Destiny*, set largely in Soho, will follow in due course.

Production of this book has been made possible with the help of the following individuals and organisations who subscribed in advance:

Neil Atkinson
Peter Bamfield
Chris Beckett
Lillian Blakey
Andrew Brewerton
Ian Brinton
Jasper Brinton
Peter Brown
Robert Caserio
John Cayley
Claire Crowther
Elaine Edwards
Allen Fisher/Spanner
Jim Goar
Giles Goodland
Fred Grand
Penny Grossi
John Hall
Andrew Hamilton
Randolph Healy/Wild Honey Press
Peter Hughes

Kristoffer Jacobson
Graeme Jukes
Richard Makin
Michael Mann
Alan Marley
Askold Melnyczuk
David Miller
John Olson
Merle Olson
Sean Pemberton
Lou Rowan
James Russell
Maurice Scully
Pablo Seoane Rodríguez
Valerie Soar
Lloyd Swanton
Eileen Tabios
Visual Associations
Keith Washington
Alastair Wilson
Anonymous x 2

www.grandiota.co.uk

www.ingramcontent.com/pod-product-compliance
Lightning Source LLC
Chambersburg PA
CBHW020112180626
46812CB00006B/2560